Knight & Play

AN EROTIC NOVEL

KITTY FRENCH

BOOKS BY THIS AUTHOR:

Knight & Play
Knight & Stay
Knight & Day, coming December 2013
Wanderlust

Kitty also writes under the pseudonym Kat French

Undertaking Love
Blaze

Chapter One

"How can I make my CV more interesting, Kara? Even *I* wouldn't employ me if this landed on my desk." Sophie sighed and flipped the paper around on the small café table for her friend to read.

"So sex it up a bit, then. Everyone does it." Kara ripped the top off a packet of sugar and shook it over the froth on her cappuccino. She scanned the CV as she twirled the long wooden stirrer around in her cup. "Take this sentence here. You say: I have worked as a personal assistant for ten years for a company director."

Sophie shrugged. "Well I have."

"Yes, *I* know that," Kara said, as if she were talking to a child. "But you have to make it sound cooler. Sexier. More fun."

"It isn't cool," Sophie snorted. "Or sexy. Or fun. I spend most of my time typing up estimates for double glazing and fending off Derek's wandering hands."

"Work with me here, Soph," Kara sighed. "What's the job you're applying for?"

"Another manager's PA role, but it's a much bigger company."

"Another building firm?"

"Umm, no." Sophie stalled.

"Well what *do* they do, then? We can tailor your CV to whatever their business is."

Sophie leaned in and lowered her voice so that no one else in the café would overhear. "It's in the adult entertainment industry."

Kara's dark eyebrows shot into her heavy fringe as she started to laugh. "Holy cow, Soph! That's some career move. Does Dan know?"

Sophie shook her head. Dan was away for a couple of days on business yet again, and it somehow hadn't felt appropriate to tell him about the job advert over the phone. She could have told him before he'd left, of course, but he'd seemed busy and distant. If she were to be completely honest, she was holding off telling him unless it came to the point where she was actually offered the job. Why rock the boat unless she needed to?

Kara frowned. "How the hell am I going to spin the sex industry into your experience with a building company?"

"I have no clue." Sophie bit the end off the flake from her hot chocolate and started to laugh. "You could always say I'm experienced with erections."

Kara grinned and pulled her laptop out of her bag. "Now you're talking. Come on. Let's see what we can do."

A couple of hours and two large frosted blueberry muffins later, Sophie slid her new, sexed-up CV into its envelope and dropped it into the postbox with a kiss for good luck.

Lucien Knight dropped the foul plastic cup of coffee from the vending machine into the waste paper basket and glanced over the CVs that had arrived in the morning's mail. If any of them happened to mention their coffee making skills, they'd just earned themselves an automatic pass to the interview stages to be his new PA.

Too old. The first CV followed his coffee into the bin.

Young kids. The second one followed the first.

It wasn't that he was ageist, or unsupportive of mothers. It was simply that he wanted a PA who would make him their number one priority, and in his experience, older women tried to mother him and young mothers were too distracted mothering someone else to make him number one on their list.

The third envelope seemed to be sealed with traces of lipstick, which was no bad thing in his book.

Sophie Black. She passed the age test, and made no reference to kids, or to a husband either for that matter. She did however, make a great deal of her excellent personal skills, and she'd made sure to mention how extremely open she was to new ideas. Girls who were extremely open to new ideas interested him a lot, as did girls who sealed their envelopes with a kiss. Despite the fact that Sophie Black didn't allude to her coffee making skills, he filed her CV on the interview pile anyway.

"Kara! I've got an interview for that PA job at Knight Inc.," Sophie whispered into her mobile. She glanced towards the office door where she could see Derek and one of the site foremen engaged in a heated discussion.

"No way! That's hilarious!" Kara hissed back, obviously equally as unable to chat but desperate for the gossip.

As soon as the thick cream envelope bearing the Knight Inc. logo had landed on the doormat next to a ruck of brown bills that morning, Sophie had felt an undeniable fizz of excitement. Dan had glanced up from his newspaper as she'd come back into the kitchen with the mail in her hand.

"Anything interesting?"

"Not really. Bills. Flyers." She'd dropped it on the work surface. "You know, junk."

He'd looked down again before she'd even finished speaking, and for once she'd been glad of his disinterest.

"So when is it?" Kara whispered in her ear.

"After work on Monday. What should I wear do you think?"

"Err, a French maid's outfit? Naughty nurse?" Kara's laugh was pure smut down the phone line.

"I'm being serious, Kara. They'll be expecting someone cool and sophisticated, and my wardrobe consists of a uniform of deathly dull chain store work suits."

"Then you'd better thank your lucky stars you've got me," Kara laughed. "I'll come over on Sunday and sort you out."

"You're a life saver." Sophie said, bolstered by her friend's support. "I'll get the wine in. Dan's away again for ten days from tomorrow so we'll have the house to ourselves."

"You're on, chick. Gotta go." Kara mumbled. "Tosser Boss is eyeballing me."

Several hours later, Sophie tipped a pre-bagged salad into a bowl and splashed a little dressing over it as she placed it in the middle of the dining table. A soft smile touched her lips as she laid a hand against the cool wood. Large and oak, she could well remember the day some years ago when she'd brought Dan a new tie and re-enacted Pretty Woman for him when he'd arrived home. He'd loosened his tie at the sight of her in just stilettos and his gift, and they'd christened the dining table, swiftly followed by the stairs.

Thinking back now, Sophie could barely believe it had ever happened.

Who were those people?

Dan had swept her off her feet from the first moment she met him, and when he proposed to her on her twenty-first birthday she hadn't needed to think twice. Sure, they were young, but they were in love, and any attempts at guidance from their families fell on stony ground. And for the most part, it worked. Wasn't it true for all long-term relationships that the excitement slows down once the first flush of lust fades away? Sophie had read enough magazine articles to know that she was in the majority when it came to having a love life that was more about routine than spontaneous sex on the dining table. And, if the truth be told, it probably wasn't all Dan's fault. Sophie knew she could just as easily be the one to instigate something, but what? And when? Dan was away so much that he could officially be classed as a part time husband, if such a role existed.

Which by default made Sophie a part time wife. The thought unsettled her, and she still had a frown on her face when Dan came through the door a few moments later.

"All right, babe?" He dropped a kiss on her forehead as he deposited his briefcase on the floor.

Sophie smiled and forced her melancholy mood aside. Tonight was their last night together for ten days; it wasn't the moment to rock the boat. "I'm fine," she said. "Hungry? I made pizza."

Dan shrugged out of his suit jacket and headed for the stairs. "Sure. Let me just go and get out of these and I'm all yours."

Sophie sliced the pizza and put wine on the table, and she smiled when Dan came down in old jeans and a white T-shirt. His hair was still shower-damp, and his feet were bare. These were the times when he felt like he was hers again, the few and far between occasions when he didn't have his suit on and his Blackberry glued against his ear. His rapid promotion through the ranks at work had been champagne moments at home, but every increment in wages had brought with it more responsibility and more travel.

"This is nice." He nodded his approval at the table, complete with candlelight.

"I thought we could use a little romance."

Dan laughed and reached for the wine bottle. "Steady on, Soph. I'm bloody knackered."

Sophie's smile faltered as she slid the pizza onto their plates. "Eat your dinner then. Get your strength back."

Dan reached for his knife and fork and launched into a work-related story as they ate, and Sophie pushed her salad around with ever increasing despondency. The evening was ebbing away from them on a tide of meaningless chitchat, when she'd really wanted to make it into something more memorable to get them through the coming days. He reached for more pizza, and Sophie took advantage of the lull to change the subject.

"I've got a job interview on Monday."

Dan looked up in surprise. "I didn't realise you were serious about looking for something else."

"I wasn't really. It just caught my eye."

Dan topped up their wine glasses. "What is it?"

Sophie hesitated. "Another PA role, just a bigger company."

"Cool." Dan yawned and rolled his shoulders. "Christ, I ache. This job's killing me, Soph."

"Yet you don't want to leave," Sophie said, pointedly. Dan moaned incessantly about his long hours, but she knew perfectly well that he wouldn't be scouring the job ads for something else.

Dan shrugged and pushed his plate away. "I'm done. Better go and pack."

Sophie nodded with a tight smile as she picked up the empty plates, then blew out the candle with a resigned huff as he disappeared. While she cleared down the kitchen, she reasoned with herself. She'd tried subtlety with her comment about gathering his strength and it had slipped under his radar. She took a good swig of wine and decided to up the ante a little. After all, it wasn't fair to expect him to make all the moves. She flicked out the light in the kitchen and mussed her hair up in the hall mirror, then added a slick of lip-gloss to her mouth for good measure.

She could hear him zipping his bag upstairs, so she skipped into the lounge and sat down, her legs tucked beneath her in a 'sit next to me' kind of way. Glancing down at her blouse, she popped a button to give Dan a bird's eye view of her lace bra when he joined her on the sofa.

Except he didn't. He gave her a distracted smile when he came down and flopped down in his armchair, then reached out and swiped the TV remote from the coffee table. "Anything good on?"

Sophie tried to ignore the sting of resentment and reached for her wine glass with a neutral smile. "I'm not sure."

Dan flicked the channel from the programme Sophie had half decided to watch and settled on a re-run of a reality cop show that she really couldn't stand the sight of.

"All packed and ready to go?" she asked.

"Think so." Dan didn't look away from the screen as he answered her.

"Ten nights is a long time," she said softly.

Dan flicked his eyes at Sophie and grinned. "Will you miss me?"

Sophie nodded. "Of course." She paused, crippled with awkwardness. "Shall we, umm, have an early night?"

"Yeah," Dan yawned. "You go on up if you like, I'll lock up and be up in five."

Sophie unwound herself off the sofa and picked up their wine glasses. As she passed Dan's chair, she leaned down and brushed a kiss over his mouth. "See you in bed."

Upstairs, she undressed slowly, leaving her lace underwear on for Dan to remove. In bed, she propped herself up and sipped her wine whilst she waited. After five minutes she fidgeted with her underwear and wondered if it looked too obvious and she should change into something else. After ten minutes she decided to pick up a book to pass the time. After twenty, she was battling to keep her eyelids open, so she gave up waiting and padded downstairs. Dan was still in the armchair, fast asleep with his Blackberry in his hand. She touched his shoulder, and he started awake and dropped his phone.

"Fuck. Sorry, Soph." He hurriedly grabbed his phone and checked the screen. Sophie turned and headed back to bed, still holding onto hope despite the fact that he'd barely so much as glanced her way as she'd stood in front of him in the underwear she'd kept on just for his benefit. She may as well have had her winter coat on.

When he came into their bedroom a few minutes later, he stripped off and slid straight into bed, grumbling as he set the alarm for earlier than usual. He flicked the lamp out and flopped back with the duvet pulled up to his chin.

Sophie turned to him in the darkness, and for a couple of minutes neither of them spoke.

She could see his profile clearly now that her eyes had adjusted to the shadows, and even though his eyes were already closed, she reached out and stroked his cheek. He turned his face into her hand and kissed her palm.

"Night, sweetheart," he murmured. "I'll try not to wake you in the morning."

Creeping desperation forced Sophie onwards, even though she was struggling to ignore Dan's fairly clear signals that he wasn't up for anything but sleep. She snuggled in close and kissed the side of his mouth. "I'm really going to miss you."

Dan sighed. "You too, babe." He shifted a little and kissed her forehead rather than her lips. "I'll be back before you know it." He laughed softly and turned over, leaving her looking at his back. "Look on the bright side, Soph. You can have sole custody of the remote while I'm gone."

Chapter Two

"Mr. Knight will see you now."

Sophie flickered a nervous smile at the immaculately dressed woman in front of her. She'd spent most of the day at work running through potential answers for possible questions that might be thrown at her, but one glimpse of the glossy, black Knight Inc. Building had chased all of her carefully memorised words out of her head. Its predatory presence on the busy road intimidated the hell out of her, and she'd seriously considered turning away.

She already had a job. She didn't need another one.

Then she'd caught sight of her reflection in the mirrored glass. Kara had been true to her word and waved her magic wand yesterday, leaving Sophie barely able to recognise the sexy, sophisticated woman gazing back at her. The jacket of the dark business suit nipped right in at the waist and then followed close against her curves. The pencil skirt ended just a hair's breadth from being too short, and her Mary Jane high heels added at least three inches to her legs. Kara was a designer clothes junkie, and she'd turned up with an armful of work clothes that were a world away from Sophie's off the peg, ordinary attire. The moment she'd slid into the deep inky purple suit, something extraordinary happened. She wasn't just Sophie, the local builder's PA any more. She was an enhanced version of herself, someone sassy and sophisticated. Someone brand new, open to endless possibilities.

Much of that confidence had drained away as she'd sat in the reception on the top floor waiting to be called through, and she could just as easily have bolted as follow the woman along the plush carpet of the corridor.

She felt physically sick.

But then they came to a halt in front of a door at the end, and after tapping it once, the woman opened it and stood aside so she could go through.

Sophie swallowed hard and stepped inside.

In the usual course of things, Sophie didn't lust after other men. But from the moment she stepped inside that room, she couldn't take her eyes off Lucien Knight.

This wasn't the usual course of things.

Tall, dark and handsome was nowhere near the mark. He was tall, definitely, but with dirty blonde hair and flint blue eyes that were now fixed on her with a predatory look of interest. He wasn't exactly in business dress, either. He might have been, earlier in the day, but right now he was down to a close-fitting charcoal shirt with the cuffs turned back to reveal strong, tanned forearms. He'd loosened his equally dark tie and popped his top button, and if he'd put his feet up on the desk and produced a glass of whisky, Sophie wouldn't have been altogether surprised. He looked like he'd tumbled out of a club, or stepped straight from the centre-fold of a glossy hipster magazine. Or in fact, make that a top shelf one.

"Come in, Ms. Black. I won't bite."

She walked across the room.

"… unless you want me to?" he murmured as an afterthought, and raised an eyebrow at her as she took a seat opposite him at the desk.

It certainly wasn't a question Sophie had devised an answer for in her interview preparation. Was she supposed to respond, or pretend she hadn't heard? Thankfully, as she considered it, Mr. Knight moved on.

"So, Ms. Black. Why do you want to be my PA?"

Phew. Safer territory. A question she had prepared for.

"Well, I've been in my current position for several years, and I feel like I need a new challenge." She watched him watching her. Her words seemed to amuse him.

"I see," he nodded. "But why here, specifically? Why Knight Incorporated?"

Sophie crossed her ankles and knotted her fingers in her lap to stop them from fidgeting. "Well… because it's very different from what I do at the moment." *Hah.* That was the understatement of the year. He was still watching her intently, but his expression gave nothing away. "And because… because, well, to be perfectly honest, I'm bored, Mr. Knight." His eyes flickered, letting her know she'd finally said something that surprised him. A silence stretched out between them as he seemed to weigh up her words.

"Do you know why I called you in for interview?" he asked, eventually.

Sophie stalled. "My CV?"

He nodded. "You sealed it with a kiss. I wanted to see the lips that made that mark."

His answer knocked the breath clean out of her lungs and sent hot prickles shooting up her neck. This was beginning to feel less like an interview and more like someone coming on to her in a bar, and that hadn't happened to her in some considerable time.

"You blush too easily, Ms. Black." He twirled a pen in his fingers. "Trust me, that's not a good thing in this industry."

His mouth twisted to one side, that assessing look still in his eyes. "This isn't an industry for shy girls." He leaned forwards on his elbows and steepled his fingers. "Are you a shy girl, Sophie?"

Jeez this was ridiculous. Sophie couldn't tell if he was making fun of her, and a fair part of her brain was shouting at her to hightail it out of the building back to the safety of her ordinary, mundane life. But something held her in her chair, and that same something gave her the boldness to meet his challenging look and answer his question.

"No, Mr. Knight. I'm not especially shy."

"It's Lucien."

Lucien. Crap. Even his name was sexy.

"Okay Sophie. Here's the deal. I need someone who can do all the usual PA stuff. You already know what that is so I won't bore you with a list, but it includes making a decent cup of coffee. Is that a problem for you?"

Sophie shook her head and laughed, almost giddy with relief. Emboldened, she replied, "That's a little chauvinistic of you, Mr. Knight."

"Lucien."

"Okay, well… for the record, yes. I make a mean cup of coffee, Lucien." Sophie tasted his name for the first time and felt as if she'd said something far dirtier.

"I'll need you to accompany me to meetings, exhibitions, the odd commercial trip. I keep odd hours. Will that bother you?"

He was all business now, and the look on his face brooked no argument. Sophie frowned. Her first thought was for Dan, but then didn't he give exactly the same service to his boss without a thought for her?

"Not a problem," she said smoothly.

"So far, so good." He nodded in approval, and scrubbed a hand over his chin for a few seconds as he studied her.

"I don't know, Sophie. You tick all the boxes, and yet…"

"Yet what?" Sophie asked. His hesitation chased away any attempt to stay businesslike. Besides, he'd already veered so far away from businesslike that it seemed unlikely to worry him.

He cocked his head to one side. 'How can I put this delicately?" He licked his lips. "You look too… innocent."

Sophie shook her head. "I'm not sure what you mean."

He threw his hands out to the sides. "This is the sex industry. Sophie. You'd be a long way from typing up building quotes here. One day you might be working on a report comparing sex toys. The next you might be ordering new cages for one of the clubs.

I need someone who can do all of that without turning a hair." Sophie knew that the telltale colour was back in her cheeks. "Someone who won't blush at the mere mention of a vibrator," he added, to illustrate his point.

"I can do all that," Sophie insisted, feeling far from certain that she could.

Lucien gave her an assessing look and opened the desk drawer.

He placed an object down on the desk between them. "What's that?" he asked. Sophie looked down and felt heat slap her cheeks again.

"Mr. Knight…" He raised an eyebrow. "Lucien… I…"

"You what, Sophie? You don't know what it is, or you're too prudish to say it?" He picked up the blue jelly silicone ring and held it out to her. Sophie looked at him, and his eyes told her that this was the acid test. Fail it, and she was out the door. She took it from him, and swallowed hard at the feel of the small, stretchy ring in her hands. She looked him squarely in the eye.

"Fine. It's a cock ring."

"Good girl," he grinned. "And what does it do?"

Sophie swallowed again and looked down. She had no intimate knowledge to draw on here.

"It… umm…"

"Wrong answer, Sophie." He frowned. "Try again."

Sophie squirmed in her chair. "I'm not totally sure, but I think it would probably make a man last longer?"

Lucien's mouth twisted to the side. "Not totally sure, huh? Am I to draw from that that you have no direct experience of sex toys?"

"Mr. Knight…" Sophie gasped. "I really don't think that's an appropriate question for any job interview." She bristled, partly with indignation and partly because he was bang on the money.

"Maybe not, but you don't want this job if you're in any way prudish."

"I am not prudish. For God's sake, I'm no blushing virgin, I'm a married woman."

For a second, Lucien looked genuinely taken aback and his eyes flickered to her left hand. "You're married?"

"Is that against the law in this industry too?"

"No, no." His whole demeanour had changed unreadably. "Tell me, what does your husband think of you applying for this job?"

Sophie faltered and her gaze slid away from his. "He's fine with it."

Lucien let out a low whistle. "He doesn't know, does he?"

"Yes. Sort of." She glanced down at her wedding ring. "He knows I have an interview, just not what it's for, exactly."

"And would he mind, do you think? I'd mind if you were my wife." Lucien's blue eyes locked on Sophie's as his words did thrilling things to her insides. If only Dan were as territorial.

"He won't mind," she said quietly. "He's pretty busy with his own work. If I'm happy, I'm sure he'll be happy."

"And are you happy, Sophie?"

She wasn't sure what he meant by the question, and it unnerved her. Were her marital problems written all over her face? Or was he simply asking if his abrasive, unique interview style bothered her? Either way, there was only one possible acceptable reply.

"Yes, I think I am."

Lucien nodded and drummed his fingers on the desk.

"Good." His smile didn't quite touch his eyes. "Thanks for coming in, Sophie. I'll be in touch." He pushed his chair backwards.

Sophie stared at him, surprised. That was it? He'd finished?

She got the distinct feeling that he'd decided she was a bad bet, and because it was unlikely she would ever see him again, she threw caution to the wind.

"You've decided I'm unsuitable."

He leaned back in his chair with a frank expression on his face. "I don't think this job is for you." He shrugged. "You're too vanilla."

"Vanilla?" She couldn't keep the note of frustration from her voice. "What does that even mean?"

He shook his head with a small laugh. "Exactly." He leaned forward and sighed. "Look, Sophie. You seem like a nice girl. But I don't need a nice girl for this job. I need someone free of inhibitions. Someone who knows their dildos from their anal beads. Someone who won't stumble like a schoolgirl if they need to say a rude word."

Sophie squared her shoulders. "You underestimate me, Lucien. I could do this job. I'm damn good, and I'm a fast learner." She held his blue gaze and willed him to believe her. It had suddenly become crucial to her that he didn't write her off as a prude, because it endorsed all of her negative feelings about her relationship with Dan. Was she really the little mouse they both seemed to take her for?

"Okay." Lucien folded his arms across his chest, and Sophie's eyes were drawn to the way his shirt defined his biceps.

"Say clitoris, Sophie."

Sophie's mouth fell open in shock. Hearing Lucien Knight unexpectedly say the word clitoris made the bottom drop out of her stomach. No way was she going to say it back just to amuse him.

"Well, that's certainly a question that didn't feature on any of the job websites I studied," she quipped to cover her embarrassment.

"You're right." He nodded in acceptance and worked the knot on his tie open. *Was he hot?* She was definitely feeling the heat in here. He tapped his pen on the desk. "Fair enough, don't say clitoris." She sighed with relief. "Say masturbation instead."

Sophie couldn't take anymore. Lucien Knight was too much. Too sexual, too arrogant, too male. Even though he was fully clothed, sex oozed from every pore of the man in a way Sophie had never encountered before. He made her think of Viking warriors, and right now she felt like a damsel in serious distress. Lucien Knight was right. She *wasn't* equipped for the candid conversations he required. She *couldn't* be as brazen as he needed her to be. She got to her feet.

"You know what, Mr. Knight? You're probably right. I'm not cut out for this." She swung her bag over her shoulder and ignored the spark of amusement in his eyes. "I'm sorry to have wasted your time."

Lucien got to his feet too and crossed to open the door. "On the contrary, Sophie. It's been my pleasure."

He'd placed himself between Sophie and the exit, leaving her no choice but to brush close to him as she left. He was a good head and shoulders taller than she was even in her high heels, and she caught the scent of him as she drew level. *Delicious.* He smelled of warm spice and citrus, and something else. Something dark and sexy, so uniquely Lucien Knight that it kicked her senses into overdrive. She wanted to leave, and yet at the same time she wanted him to say something to stop her.

She turned to him, and found him leaning on the doorjamb with a lazy smile on his face.

"Goodbye, Mr. Knight."

"Ms. Black." He inclined his head, but made no further move, leaving her no option but to walk away.

Except for one.

Sophie turned away, and then swung back around and said something that she never imagined she'd say as part of a job interview.

"Clitoris." She took pleasure in watching the predatory spark re-ignite in his cool blue eyes, and she licked her lips before she spoke again. "Masturbation."

Sophie met his gaze head on, dizzy with exhilaration.

"Cock rings. Anal beads. Vibrators, dildos and…" she cast around desperately in her limited imagination for a big finish, "and blow up dolls!"

The amused heat in Lucien eyes scorched her. In that moment she wasn't ordinary Sophie Black, builder's PA and invisible wife. She was sexy and sophisticated Ms. Black, able to stop Viking sex-gods in their tracks with just a few little words. She noticed the way Lucien's throat worked as he swallowed before he spoke.

"You start in the morning. Nine o' clock sharp. Don't be late, Ms. Black."

Later that evening, curled up on the sofa eating Chinese from plates balanced on their knees, Kara stared at Sophie, agog. "You aren't actually going to take the job though, right?"

Sophie tucked her feet underneath her and nodded. "Kara, I am. I have to." She took a sip of her wine and searched for the words to explain her feelings. "If I don't, then I'm accepting that this is as exciting as my life is ever going to get." She gestured round her lounge. "A dead-end job, a husband who's barely here and doesn't notice me when he is…"

"Soph, if you've got problems with Dan, this job is only going to make them a million times worse, you know?"

"It won't. Maybe I'll learn stuff to spice things up for us."

"Can't you just talk to him?"

"Kara, I'm not taking this job because of what's going on with me and Dan. I'm taking it because for a while back there today I glimpsed a different version of myself, and I liked her better."

Kara shook her head and laughed in resignation. "You'd better hang onto those other clothes then. Something tells me you're going to need them."

Sophie locked all the doors and went to bed with her mobile in her hand to call Dan. She listened to the clicks as it made the long distance connection, and it rang out once or twice before it diverted to his answer phone. She glanced at her watch. It was just after ten thirty for her, so a little after midnight for him. Who was he with that he should need to reject her call at that time? He wasn't due to start his meetings until tomorrow. Sophie sighed and slid into bed, her mobile still clutched in her hand in case he called back.

He didn't.

Chapter Three

At eight fifty the next morning, Sophie passed through the black, gleaming doors of Knight Inc. with her heart in her mouth.

Poor old Derek had never sounded so lost for words as when she'd called him last night out of the blue to resign, and thankfully he'd been too flustered to argue with her request to use holiday days owed in lieu of the company's one week notice policy.

Her old boss was a letch of the highest order; Sophie pitied the next girl who would have to put up with his wandering hands.

Was her new boss a letch? Lucien Knight loomed large in her mind, a bronzed, muscled warrior with sparkling blue eyes and a killer way with words. *No.* He wasn't a letch. His job just demanded that the usual veil of decency be removed. Even though Sophie had only met Lucien once, she already sensed she could trust him not to cross the line. Derek hadn't been able to keep his grubby old hands off her, but Sophie felt pretty certain that Lucien Knight wouldn't lay an untoward finger on her.

Unless he thought she wanted him to.

Sophie shook her head to dislodge the unbidden thought, and stepped out of the elevator onto the plush carpet of the top floor.

The same immaculate woman as yesterday inhabited reception, but her smile was a fraction warmer today as Sophie approached the desk.

"Mr. Knight is expecting you, Sophie. Welcome aboard."

Sophie smiled, disconcerted that the woman knew her name

already. "Thank you." The receptionist tapped the keyboard and made no move to get up. "Shall I just go on through?"

In answer the woman nodded and extended an arm behind her towards the corridor.

That was that, then. She was now officially an employee at Knight Inc.

Nerves swirled low in Sophie's stomach as she approached Lucien's door at the end of the swathe of carpet. Yesterday already felt as if she'd dreamed it – things like that didn't happen in real life, did they? In books maybe, or films, but not to ordinary girls leading ordinary lives. Except it *had* happened, and as Sophie tapped twice on Lucien's door, she felt like anything but an ordinary girl.

"Come in." His quiet command filtered through the door, and she turned the handle and stepped inside.

"Sophie." A lazy smile crossed his mouth when he looked up. "You came."

She raised her eyebrows in surprise. "Did you expect me not to?"

He shrugged. "How could you resist?"

Sophie smiled despite her nerves. She couldn't help it. Lucien Knight was just about the most self-assured - no, in fact, cocky - man she'd ever met.

"This way." Lucien stood and opened a door to a second room to one side of his desk. Sophie hadn't noticed the doorway until now, and she crossed behind his desk to stand alongside him. The adjoining office was smaller, with the same lush decoration and picture window views of London as Lucien enjoyed.

"You should find everything you need in here. Claire has left detailed guidance notes."

"Claire?" Sophie's interest was piqued.

"My previous PA. She had to leave a couple of weeks earlier than planned, but you should find everything in order."

Sophie wasn't brave enough to ask why Claire had needed to make a speedy exit. Maybe she'd fallen for her boss…

"Why don't you take a little time to get acquainted with things? And I'll call you if I need anything."

Lucien left Sophie's door open and sat down at his desk. Despite what he'd just said to the contrary, he'd have put down good money that Sophie Black wouldn't turn up this morning. She'd surprised him again, just as she had when she'd turned back yesterday and said things that clearly made her uncomfortable. He sensed the spunky girl lurking beneath her good girl demeanour, and he was looking forward to helping her find her way out. He looked up as she appeared in the doorway.

"Coffee, Mr. Knight?" There was a gleam in her eye that could almost be deemed mischievous.

"Why, thank you, Sophie. I'd like that very much. Espresso, if you can work that infernal machine out."

She disappeared again, and he could hear the clank of the high-tech coffee machine in her office that he'd never bothered to get to grips with. A few minutes later she placed a steaming cup down on the desk next to him.

"I wasn't sure if you took sugar," she said, a sachet in her hand in readiness.

"No, thank you. That's perfect."

She inclined her head, and sunlight bounced off the clip that held her hair up. Lucien's fingers itched to reach out and remove it, to let her blonde hair fall around her face. How long was it, he wondered? Shoulder length? Long enough to cover her breasts? He shifted in his seat, suddenly uncomfortable.

He picked up the cup and watched her retreat into her office. He had much to learn about Sophie Black, but two things were already apparent. The girl had a fabulous backside, and she could indeed make a mean cup of coffee.

Sophie sat down at the large, unfamiliar desk and touched a key on the computer keyboard. The screen instantly lit up, the Knight Inc. logo emblazoned across it.

Claire had indeed been very thorough with her handover notes, Sophie found everything listed from computer passwords to intricate details of how to manage Lucien's diary. The thought of being in charge of the movements of the six foot sex god sitting outside her door set off the nerves in her stomach again, so she entered the computer passwords and opened up the email programme. It seemed as good a place to start as any.

The next couple of hours passed in a blur, and almost to her surprise, Sophie found that the job actually held some similarities to her old one. She still had to clear emails, manage the post, type memos. She drew strength from those familiarities. *I can do this.*

She was about to get to grips with the filing systems when an instant message box popped up in the corner of the screen.

"You're very industrious in there, Ms. Black. I'm impressed."

A smile touched the corners of her mouth. How very Lucien Knight to choose to do something other than just lean back far enough to put his head around the door and speak to her. She was fast learning that he was a man who avoided the predictable. Her fingers hovered over the keyboard as she tried to decide how to respond. First and foremost, this man was her boss. She should just be screamingly professional, but he'd somehow managed to show her that that wasn't what he was looking for from her.

She rather thought that he wanted the other Sophie. Even so, there was something inherently intimate about messaging him that made her feel weird. But turned on weird, rather than run for the hills weird.

She racked her brain. What would the other Sophie say?

"I aim to please, Mr. Knight."

She pressed send.

A few seconds later, his reply flashed in.

"Then I hope you're a good shot, Sophie."

Sophie laughed softly under her breath.

"I never miss. Is there anything particular you'd like me to do next, Mr. Knight?"

"Yes. I want you to call me Lucien."

Sophie blushed. She'd already attempted to call him Lucien a few times that morning, but his name felt wrong in her mouth. Why couldn't he have a run of the mill name? Something normal, like Tom, or Jack... *or Dan.* Something that could have been anyone's, rather than a name that was so personally, completely his? He seemed to fill every corner of the word.

He chose that moment to roll his chair back and come through into the office with a sheaf of papers in his hand.

"Sophie, could you work on these after lunch, please?" He handed the papers over. "It's customer feedback reports from our product testing group. I need the results collating, please."

She put the papers aside with a professional smile. *Say his name. Say his name.* "Of course... Lucien." There. She'd said it, and no one had died.

His eyes glittered with approval. "Much better."

He glanced at his watch. "I have to go out for an hour or two. Don't forget to take a lunch break."

He left a few minutes later, and Sophie breathed out properly for the first time since she'd arrived that morning. She'd been tense, too tense in his presence. An unbidden image of Lucien Knight massaging the tension out of her shoulders popped into her mind, and she pushed it aside hurriedly. What was happening to her? Her last boss had never unsettled her like this, but then Derek was a man whose attentions she had actively avoided, rather than daydreamed about like a star struck fan-girl. The fact was that being around Lucien Knight had her on edge.

She'd never met anyone like him before. He radiated a raw sexual energy; it dripped from his every pore. He had exempted himself from the usual conventions that shackle people and had created the Knight Inc. empire on the back of it. Her pre-interview research had told her little of the man himself, but much about the multi- million pound business of adult clubs and stores he operated up and down the UK. He seemed to view the world through an x-rated lens, and he had made his millions by tapping into the vein of depravity that ran through every otherwise decent person.

Up until now, Sophie had considered herself a conventional woman. Accepting this job was probably – no, definitely - the biggest risk she'd ever taken. She'd applied for it because the boredom of her life was suffocating her, and so far it seemed that if her aim had been to inject some excitement into her days, she'd scored a spectacular goal.

Was she escaping from her old life? Yes.

Was she using the job to stop herself from thinking about the terse text she'd received from Dan this morning, telling her not to call so late again and that he'd be in touch when he could? Absolutely.

He'd been gone for three days and had yet to find the time to take her calls. Not that that was so unusual these days. It had been that way on more and more overnight trips over the last couple of years.

Sophie knew better than to let herself think about it too deeply, because then there would be questions that needed answers. Up until now she hadn't wanted to ask them, even though they were there in huge black capital letters. The gulf between them had slowly widened into an ocean awash with the flotsam and jetsam of a neglected relationship; countless cold shoulders instead of enveloping hugs. Too many dry pecks on the cheek rather than passionate clinches on the dining table. Too many hurriedly hidden text messages. The circumstantial evidence all pointed towards another woman, and Sophie's sexual confidence had ebbed away in the face of Dan's undeniable rebuttals in bed. She'd been feeling old, and cold. Until now. Until she'd stepped into Lucien Knight's force field yesterday evening.

He had a way of looking at her that made her feel all woman, and Sophie could feel herself blossoming… ripening… re-emerging… and she liked it.

She liked it a lot.

She grabbed her lunch from her bag and returned to her desk to make a start on that report Lucien had asked for. She flipped the file open, and the full-page illustration on page one stilled her sandwich half way to her mouth.

What was that? She tilted her head to the side to try to work it out but ended up none the wiser. A standard vibrator given to her on her hen night was as far as her experience with sex toys went, and even that hadn't seen much use. Sophie flicked over the page and read the product description.

The all new Vibrating Lick'n'Love Ring features all the best features of our regular vibrating cock ring, with the addition of an innovative silicone tongue-shaped clit stimulator for enhanced couple play. Designed to move and feel like a real tongue, the remote control Lick'n'Love Ring combines the best of all worlds. The fully waterproof unit also comes with detachable anal stimulation beads for male or female use.'

Sophie read the blurb with her hands pressed against her cheeks in shock. Was Lucien testing her again?

Or was this just the reality of the job she'd taken on? Sophie wasn't certain, but either way she needed to write the report. A flick through the rest of the pages showed them to be individual satisfaction surveys with tick box answers, and then a space for individual comments. Straightforward enough to collate, but far from easy to read. Sophie found herself growing hot and flustered as she read the anonymous strangers' responses on the forms. It certainly seemed as if the toy had found favour with its reviewers.

Mind blowing orgasm, one said. *Felt just like a real tongue,* another reported. Sophie found her eyes constantly pulled back to the image of the toy as she tallied up the responses.

Was it really that good? How life-like would it actually feel? These questions and more crossed Sophie's mind as she collated the comments, and she didn't hear Lucien's office door open until he appeared around her doorway. He gave her a mock salute when she glanced up.

Were her cheeks telltale red? Could he see how flustered she was? By the knowing gleam in his blue eyes, probably yes.

"I'll be just out here if you need anything," he murmured.

Sophie looked up as he turned away, and couldn't help but notice the way his dark shirt clung to the width of his shoulders. He was obviously in great shape, long and lean with defined muscles. Sophie puffed her fringe out of her eyes and shook her head to dislodge her mind from the path it was heading down. A path that had her wondering just how good Lucien Knight would look without that shirt on.

"How's the report coming along?" The question appeared in the chat box in the corner of the screen. She hesitated, then tapped,

"Okay I think. Almost finished."

"Nice work. Come and feedback the results to me when you're done."

Lucien probably heard her gasp out loud. The idea of discussing the reports findings with him made her squirm in her seat.

She couldn't, she just couldn't.

"Yes you can." The words popped up on the screen, and she heard his low laugh. *"Your CV said you want to be challenged, Ms. Black."*

Sophie put her hands over her face. She hadn't expected this sort of challenge.

"Fifteen minutes. Bring coffee."

Sophie almost longed for her old job as she clicked save on the last of the comments and pressed print. Boredom was easier to handle than this barrage of nerves that had her constantly on edge.

She pinned two copies of the report together and put them on the tray next to the coffee. It was now or never. She popped her head around the door.

"I could just email the report to you if you're busy?"

Lucien grinned at her last ditch avoidance pitch.

"No need. I'm all ears, Sophie."

She turned back and took a deep breath as she picked up the tray. It was time for the other Sophie to come out to play; the one Lucien had given the job to. *She could do this.*

She turned around and went through into Lucien's office.

Chapter Four

Sophie placed Lucien's coffee down next to him and took the seat opposite his at the desk.

"So, Sophie. How did you get on with the report?"

Sophie picked up the two printed copies and handed one across to him. He glanced down at the front cover, on which Sophie had included the image of the Love'n'Lick Ring and its blurb accompanied by the date and report header.

"Nice presentation." He nodded. "So far, so good."

"Thank you." Sophie smiled but didn't look up and meet his eyes. She'd decided that the only way she was going to make it through this session was by imagining that he was her old boss, Derek, and they were discussing something as innocuous as wall grouting options. If she looked up, that would be impossible.

Lucien turned the top page over to the results analysis.

"Talk me through the findings, please Sophie."

Sophie swallowed at his softly spoken command. Short of refusing, he'd left her little room for manoeuvre. She cleared her throat.

"Well, as you can see, the test group found that the product was, umm… fit for purpose."

"Fit for purpose?" Lucien's laugh was low and suggestive. "You're going to have to do better than that, Ms. Black. From the top, please."

Sophie's fingers touched against her throat, and Lucien's eyes lingered on the movement.

"Okay. Right. Well… question one. The testers were asked to

judge the product on appearance."

"And?"

"And they liked it. A couple of people would have preferred it to be coloured, but most liked the fact that it was clear."

"Why?"

"Why what?"

"Why do they prefer clear to coloured?"

"From the comments, people like the fact that it blends in rather than stands out."

Lucien nodded. "And what do you think of its appearance?"

"Me?"

Lucien nodded again and looked at her with expectant eyes, and she tried to imagine that he'd just asked her which grout mix she would recommend. It didn't work very well.

"I couldn't really say," she stumbled and flicked back to the front cover to look at it again. Lucien wheeled his chair backwards to a cabinet and opened it, then returned to the desk with a real life version of the Love'n'Lick in his hand. Sophie blanched as he took it out of the packet. He held it out across the desk, and Sophie did the only thing she could. She took it.

"Look at it," he said, and she dropped her eyes hurriedly. "Test how it feels against your skin."

Sophie could do nothing to stop the warm flush on her cheeks, but what else did he expect?

"Note how you can see your own skin through it. We designed it to become almost invisible when used."

She could hear the note of pride in his voice. However titillating the subject matter seemed, the fact was that this product research was essential information to Lucien and he took it seriously.

She looked down at the sex toy in her hand, and curiosity overtook embarrassment. It was far softer and stretchier than she'd imagined it would be, more tactile. The tongue stimulator struck her as very... well... tongue-shaped. Her mind skipped along the obvious path... how would it feel to use this during sex? And more disturbingly, it wasn't Dan who starred in her x-rated imaginary sex test.

"Question two," she coughed, and chased the images from her head. "How easy was the product to use?"

People had raved over it on the questionnaires.

"It scored highly in this area, Lucien. People found it incredibly easy to use."

"Good. That's what we hoped." He seemed satisfied with that, so she thanked her lucky stars and moved on.

"The next question was aimed specifically at women." Sophie willed her cheeks to stay cool. "It asked if the product increased the female partner's pleasure during sex."

Sophie couldn't look up. This whole conversation was too intimate. She wouldn't even have felt comfortable having it with Dan, let alone Lucien.

"And the results?"

Sophie nodded. "Umm, yes. The responses were favourable again."

"For everyone? No additional comments?"

Oh, there had been comments. Plenty of them.

Sophie passed her hand over her forehead and coughed again. This was excruciatingly hard, given the subject matter. But then wasn't that the point? This was the bread and butter of the business she was now part of, she needed to prove to Lucien that she could handle it. It was time to pull herself together and be the PA Lucien needed, or she might as well get her coat now. The thought of losing the job centred her, and she put her shoulders back and looked up.

"Every last women loved it, Lucien." Sophie spoke without allowing a trace of her inward tremble into her voice. "They all found that the additional clitoral stimulation helped them achieve orgasm during sex. One woman reported three orgasms within half an hour, and many mentioned that the tongue action felt extremely life-like."

Lucien nodded. "And you, Sophie?"

"Me?"

"Do *you* think the tongue action feels life-like?"

"Lucien, I haven't…" Sophie's eyebrows hit her fringe.

"Switch it on and test it against the palm of your hand."

"You're not serious."

"Perfectly. I need you to be fully conversant with all aspects of what we do, and that includes product awareness."

Dear God. He genuinely expected her to switch it on and test it, right here in front of him. He was outrageous, and Sophie had never felt so exposed in her life. *Or so turned on.*

She flicked the switch on the vibrating tongue, and the little machine buzzed into life in her hand. When she looked down she could see that the tongue had small raised bumps all over its surface that undulated in a wave-like motion.

A tongue-like motion. She flicked her eyes up at Lucien and found him watching her face intently, and his blue eyes had darkened to navy glitter. He raised one eyebrow at her in a challenge.

"Try it against your palm." It was more of an order than a question, but one Sophie found herself ready to comply with.

She placed the tip of the tongue lightly against the centre of her hand.

Lucien shook his head. "Not like that." He came around the desk and dropped on his haunches in front of her chair. "Imagine the position it would be in during sex." Reaching out, he placed one large, golden brown hand flat underneath her smaller one to hold it steady, and then with his other hand he turned the toy over and pressed the tongue stimulator flat against her palm.

"There. Like that," he said, looking up at her. "How does that feel now?"

Sophie sat rooted to the spot and stared down at him, wide eyed.

"Like someone is licking my palm," she all but whispered.

He flicked the switch and the vibrations increased.

"And now?"

Sophie shifted in her seat. The scent of Lucien reached her nose and filled her head with cinnamon and spice, and the warm strength of his hands holding the toy against hers made her want his hands on her everywhere else. His eyes watched their hands, and he looked somehow vulnerable with the sweep of his lashes against his cheek.

"It's licking me harder," she said.

Lucien nodded and snagged his bottom lip between his teeth. He pushed the slider onto full strength, and the little tongue started to lap urgently against Sophie's palm.

"And this, Sophie? How does this feel?"

Sophie closed her eyes. She couldn't get her breath.

"Honestly?" she breathed, her mind back on her earlier fantasy of a shirtless Lucien. "It makes me want sex... to know how it would feel between my legs." She dragged her eyes open and realised with horror that she'd actually just said that out loud. Lucien stared at her with barely controlled lust, his breathing almost as shallow as her own.

"That's excellent, Sophie."

He cleared his throat and snapped the vibrations off, giving Sophie a couple of seconds to gather herself together as he returned to his seat. "I think we can send this one to production," he said, dropping the Lick'n'Love toy into his drawer. "It seems to hit the spot perfectly."

Sophie stayed at her desk until well after five o clock, waiting for Lucien to leave before she passed through his office. She couldn't believe what had happened out there earlier, and she couldn't blame him because she'd willingly let it happen. From the moment she'd set eyes on Lucien Knight, she'd fallen.

She should resign, run for her life and her marriage before anything more serious happened.

Because it would.

The computer screen lit up as the instant messaging box popped up.

"I'm done for the evening, Ms. Black. I hope you've enjoyed your first day as much as I have."

Sophie read his words, and any thoughts of resignation melted away. *"Yes, thank you. It's been very… illuminating."*

"I hope that's a good thing. I've left some homework on my desk for you. Pick it up on your way out."

And with that, he called out goodnight and she heard his door close behind him a second or two later.

She dropped her head in her hands. *What the hell was she doing?* In the space of twenty-four hours, her life had gone from humdrum to something straight out of a top shelf movie. She picked up her bag and jacket and went out through Lucien's office, where the Lick'n'Love sex toy lay on top of a piece of paper with her name scrawled across the top.

Sophie,
Keep this. You seemed to like it.
I don't need you to start until 2pm tomorrow, expect it to be a late one.
L

A little after one the following afternoon, Lucien put the phone down and drummed his fingers on the desk. As far as he was concerned, the information he'd just learned about Sophie Black changed everything. Or the information about her husband, to be precise.

The man obviously didn't expect Sophie to check up on him, because he'd barely even bothered to cover the tracks of his two year affair. As Lucien sat and digested the information, an email pinged in from his head of security confirming the details he'd just outlined over the telephone. Lucien had learned over the years that his industry attracted more than its fair share of wacko job applicants, so any new staff were routinely vetted. Quite why he'd ordered checks to be carried out on Daniel Black as well as Sophie he couldn't easily explain, but it turned out that his instincts had been right on the money.

A series of photographs accompanied the written report on the screen. Lucien's mouth twisted in distaste at the sight of the man Sophie was apparently married to walking through Heraklion airport with his arm around a dark haired, elfin woman.

She was very different from Sophie. The man had diverse tastes. This woman was small and tanned, with severely cropped dark hair. Sophie was taller, and fairer, with curves that would no doubt be soft and full in Lucien's hands. She reminded him of a young horse: coltish, jittering between nerves and spirit, ready to be taken in hand. He'd deliberately pushed her yesterday. He could easily have read that report and drawn his own conclusions, but it was much more fun to see how far she was willing to go.

She'd surprised him, just as she had at her interview. Beneath the cool, professional exterior that he could see she was working hard to project, Lucien detected a sensual woman waiting in the wings. She was like a ripe peach that no one had bothered to pick, and he wanted to sink his teeth right in.

"Loser," he muttered under his breath as he scrolled down through pictures of the couple taken yesterday. *Yesterday.* Laughing in a bar, their heads close together. Reading by a pool, his head resting on her stomach. A nighttime shot of them wrapped around each other on their hotel balcony, and if Lucien's eyes didn't deceive him, the woman was naked.

There was no question.

Sophie's husband was cheating on her.

As far as Lucien was concerned, that rendered Sophie Black a free agent, even if she didn't know it herself.

Chapter Five

Sophie emerged from the elevator onto the top floor at just before two, dressed today in a bottle green dress that clung to her every curve. It was a dress she wouldn't have dared to wear for her old job, and for that matter wouldn't have wanted to. Being Derek's PA had been all about fending off his wandering hands, but being Lucien's PA brought with it a whole new set of parameters.

What would she do if Lucien's hands started to wander? In truth, she was starting to feel more worried that her own hands might be the ones to stray. She'd tossed and turned in her big, empty bed most of last night, her head full of fantasies of Lucien Knight giving her a personal demonstration of the Lick'n'Love toy. Although it was just as well she'd had something to concentrate her mind on, because Dan had once again proved elusive aside from a message on the answer phone waiting for her when she'd arrived home yesterday. *What was the point of calling her at home when he knew she'd be at work?* The idea that he'd done it for precisely that reason lurked in the back of her head, but she refused to allow it to come to the fore. She didn't want to have that conversation, even with herself. Dan was a busy man, and since yesterday, she'd become an extremely busy woman, too.

Sophie bypassed the reception desk today with a polite nod towards the receptionist, and a small thrill of belonging rippled low in her belly when she rapped her knuckles softly against Lucien's door.

"You don't need to knock." He was right there and opened the door wide for her to pass. Sophie stepped inside the lush office, feeling rather like a lion had opened the door of his lair and beckoned her in.

"Good afternoon, Lucien." She raised her eyes and gave him the benefit of a megawatt smile. She'd made a pact with herself as she'd applied her eye make up carefully that lunchtime. From the moment she stepped foot inside Knight Inc. today, she was going to let the other Sophie take over, and she was damn well going to enjoy it.

"Sophie," he murmured, and the slight smile on his lips let her know that her greeting had pleased him. *Christ, he was gorgeous.* All in black, from his well fitted shirt to his trousers that tapered down to black boots. He was covered from the throat down, yet somehow sexier than any other man naked.

How would Lucien look naked? The scandalous thought made Sophie glance down at her shiny shoes and hope mind reading wasn't one of Lucien's skills. Although, it wouldn't surprise her if it was. He seemed to look at her and see straight through her carefully constructed outer shell, right through to a dormant, sexy temptress that needed awakening from her slumber. She'd known Lucien Knight for less than forty-eight hours, but he'd already changed her in more ways than anyone else had in her entire life.

A few minutes later, Sophie glanced at Lucien's computer screen as she placed coffee next to him on his desk. From what she could make out, it looked like a club website, but not any kind of club she'd ever been in. It was dark and opulent, and screamed sex from every shot.

"Is that one of your clubs?"

He picked up his coffee and rolled his shoulders. "Yes. The newest of the Gateway Clubs. It's curtain up tonight." He paused and licked his lips. "We'll head over there around five o' clock."

"We?" Sophie's mouth went dry.

Lucien nodded. "Do you have a problem with that?"

Did she have a problem with that? She shook her head. "I guess not. It's just I've never been to a ..."

He laced his fingers behind his head and leaned back in his chair, a lazy grin on his face. "A what, Sophie?"

"Anywhere like that." Sophie gestured towards the screen.

"Don't worry. You'll be perfectly safe."

She glanced down at her dress. "Aren't I a little underdressed for a club?"

Lucien's laugh was low and suggestive. "Quite the opposite, actually." He laughed again at her shocked expression. "I'm joking. We're going to work, not play."

Sophie nodded and escaped back to her own office.

She didn't want to go to a sex club with him.

She did want to go to a sex club with him.

She opened the email programme and started work, letting the routine of getting to grips with her new job soothe her tattered nerves. Her predecessor had run a very tight ship, which made Sophie's job much easier and stopped her from needing to constantly ask Lucien for help. A bleep from the computer alerted her to the flashing message box on the screen.

"You're very quiet in there."

"How much noise do you expect a PA to make?"

"The previous one was quite vocal."

What did he mean by that? Sophie burned to know why Claire had needed to leave the job early. Had she been sleeping with Lucien? Had it all gone wrong? He certainly didn't seem to be nursing a broken heart.

Lost in thought, Sophie must have taken too long to reply, because a second message flashed in as she sat there mulling things over.

"She left to marry her French boyfriend. A whirlwind romance, or some equally trite phrase, I believe she used."

Christ, he really was a mind reader. Or else, he really understood how her mind worked. Sophie went through to Lucien's office and picked up his empty cup. It was half past four.

"Do we need to leave soon?"

Lucien nodded. "Don't be nervous, Sophie. I think you'll enjoy it if you keep an open mind."

Sophie appreciated his attempt to settle her nerves, but the fact that she was going to need an open mind was actually more worrying than calming.

"I'll just grab my bag." Back in her office, Sophie checked her phone for messages. Nothing. She sighed heavily. Even by Dan's standards, this was ridiculous. She flicked her mobile into mirror mode and slicked a fresh coat of gloss on her lips, then paused for a second as her reflection gazed back at her. *Did she look different, somehow? Did her eyes have a more alive glow than usual?* This job and Lucien Knight made her skin tingle with excitement and the blood flow a little faster in her veins.

"Come on Sophie. Time to roll."

An hour or so later Lucien eased his Aston Martin into a reserved parking bay outside the newest in his chain of Gateway clubs and turned to Sophie in the passenger seat.

"This is it."

She glanced out of the windscreen at the gleaming, low-slung building, and then turned big, apprehensive eyes to him.

"Is it open yet?"

"Not yet. It opens at eight."

Sophie's eyes cut to the clock on the dash. He could almost see her working out how much 'safe time' she had left.

He turned to face her. "Sophie. This is business. We aren't here to play, so just relax, okay?"

He saw her throat move as she nodded and swallowed hard. She didn't fool him for a second with her acts of bravado. She was like a kitten, brave every now and then, but mostly marshmallow. Her feisty interludes turned him on, and he wanted to push her into situations that encouraged the tigress in her to come out more often. The girl shimmered with untapped sexual potential. Her dick of a husband obviously wasn't able to see what he could see, or he wouldn't be swanning around the Med with some pixie-faced tramp.

The man must have rocks in his head, or else not be using his head at all. He was obviously the kind of guy who listened to his cock rather than his conscience.

He got out and opened Sophie's car door. "Come on. I'll give you the grand tour before it opens."

The reception area was a world away from Sophie's expectations. More like an upmarket spa than a club, she thought, as Lucien pointed out the changing rooms as they passed through the double doors beyond the reception area. Inside, the club opened out onto a large open plan space, opulently decked out in aubergine velvets and gilt chandeliers.

"This is the social area." Lucien gestured at the various seating nooks, a bar, and a dance floor.

"It looks like any other club," Sophie marvelled, surprised by the normality of the space. "Or a nicer version of a normal club."

"I'll take that." Lucien nodded. "What did you expect? Something seedy? People use this area to make friends, dance, have a drink…" He shrugged.

"Just like a normal club," Sophie said again, feeling slightly less intimidated.

"Kind of." Lucien's tone made her look back at him curiously, but he just shrugged again and motioned for her to head towards the open tread staircase that ran up one side of the dance floor.

She regretting going ahead of him as soon as she set foot on the stairs; he wouldn't be able to avoid a close-up view of her backside, and Kara's bottle green dress was cut to leave little to the imagination. She forced herself to keep climbing the steps steadily, and when she turned to him at the top he looked at her with a grin.

"What?"

He threw his hands out to the side and raised his eyebrows

innocently.

"Nothing."

Sophie narrowed her eyes at him.

"Which way next?"

Lucien placed a hand on the small of her back and urged her forwards down a corridor. The moody décor from downstairs continued up here, dark and opulently atmospheric. Each door along the corridor was closed, three on either side. Lucien reached for the first one and pushed it open, and Sophie peeped in. And then, hesitantly, stepped inside and stared.

"Okay. So this is nothing like a normal club anymore," she murmured, taking in the huge bed area in the centre of the room and the mirrored ceiling.

"No." Lucien's voice was close enough to warm her neck, and his hand still scorched the small of her back. "We choose the best fittings and fixtures to make our rooms the most comfortable around." Sophie nodded, too conscious of the fact that she was staring at a big sexy bed with Lucien to comment on the quality of the furnishings.

"Try it out. Tell me if it's comfortable."

Sophie gasped and shook her head.

"Don't panic, it's unused. This is launch night, remember?"

Sophie weighed up her options. She kind of wanted to say no, but she had to acknowledge that she kind of wanted to say yes too. She remembered her resolution to have fun today, and stepped tentatively forward towards the edge of the bed.

What would sexy Sophie do? She dropped to her knees on the edge of the mattress and crawled to the centre, then flipped onto her back and glanced up at her own reflection. She caught her breath. The woman looking back at her was nothing like the woman she usually saw. This girl was sexy, no, sexual. Rosy cheeked, blonde waves spilling over rich aubergine velvet like a fifties pin-up.

"Well?"

Lucien crossed to the bottom of the bed and gazed down at her, then reached for a button that made the whole bed vibrate.

She shot up on her elbows, and he laughed, low and smutty. "Pretty cool, huh?"

The vibrations did strange things. Sophie lay back and closed her eyes, allowing the sensations to play along her spine. She pushed her body down into them, and in answer Lucien turned up the intensity. Sophie could feel her whole body melting into the bed and as she pushed her bottom down, the sensations were strong enough to radiate all the way up between her legs. She gasped involuntarily and opened her eyes, meeting Lucien's gaze as he watched her. "Shall I turn it up again?" he asked, levelly, one knee resting on the mattress.

Sophie straightened her dress and crawled hurriedly off the bed.

"It's, umm, very comfortable," she managed, as she darted out of the room. *Jesus Christ. What was happening to her?*

She jumped as Lucien's hand returned to the small of her back. Her skin throbbed with awareness. If he'd chosen that moment to press her against the wall, she'd have let him. And begged him for more.

He opened the doors to the rest of the rooms along the corridor one by one, but Sophie made sure to do no more than stick her head around and peep inside. Which was just as well, given that one room held a cage and shackles, plus an impressive array of whips and other sinister looking things she didn't recognise on the wall. Another revealed a Nordic steam room, and a further one seemed quite tame by comparison, with its central pool table. Tame until Sophie's mind offered up the idea of Lucien bending her double over it. She caught his eye and, not for the first time, she felt as if he could see the very thoughts inside her head.

As the tour continued, Sophie became familiar with the concept of playrooms for couples, swingers, singles… whatever your desire, it could be met here in these shadowy rooms.

A large spa area dominated the rear of the upstairs space, with an opulent hot tub lit with inviting stars and glittering mirrors all the way around. It was undeniably fabulous.

"Fancy a dip?"

Sophie had to look over at Lucien to be certain he was joking. After the unexpected interlude in the first room she couldn't be altogether sure.

"Maybe later," she ventured, and received instant gratification from his expression of surprise. "Just kidding." She smiled sweetly.

"That's a shame, Princess."

Sophie caught her breath at his casual endearment. Coming from him, this towering Viking, it was mind-numbingly sexy. She was in way over her head with Lucien Knight, and in that single moment of clarity she made a decision. If she didn't let herself have this man, she'd spend her entire life wondering what would have happened if she had. Dan had absented himself from her in body and mind for long enough. *No more.*

Lucien unlocked a side door, and led her up a separate flight of stairs to his private suite on the top floor. The front area held a desk, with office paraphernalia to one side and a lounge with invitingly sumptuous sofas and a huge TV on the other. Double doors stood open at the end of the room to reveal a decadent bedroom beyond. Sophie moved silently forward to stand on the threshold, and her eyes took in the huge bed, the massive gilt-edged mirror leaning against the wall, the open door affording her a view into a hotel-style, slate tiled bathroom.

This was it.

Now or never.

Chapter Six

Sophie stepped into the bedroom and sat down on the club chair nearest to the window.

Lucien leaned one strong shoulder against the door and tilted his head to one side, watching her.

She crossed her ankles and looked up at him.

"My husband is having an affair, Lucien."

He had the grace to look genuinely shocked, then waited and watched for her to continue.

"And here's the thing. Right at this moment, he's God knows where with God knows who until next weekend, and I don't think I even care."

How good did it feel to say that? Sophie was momentarily taken aback by the strength of her relief at hearing her own words out loud. Dan had held her down with his casual disinterest for long enough. Acknowledging it was a release. Lucien crossed the room slowly, never taking his eyes off her, and sat in the chair opposite.

"He's a fucking fool."

Sophie shrugged and looked out of the window. "Maybe. He's avoided having sex with me for more than six months now."

"I'll say it again. He's a fucking fool."

"Yes."

Sophie gazed at Lucien opposite. *Jesus, he was beautiful.* If she was going to be unfaithful with anyone, this sinful, sexy man was it.

"Would it help if we fucked?"

Sophie laughed and put her hands to her cheeks in shock.

"Could we at least have a drink first?"

Lucien lifted an eyebrow at her and crossed the room to open a sleek cabinet. He returned moments later and placed a champagne bucket and two glasses on the table between them, then sat down opposite her again.

"Take your dress off," he said, softly.

Sophie caught her breath. If she'd thought she was turned on before, she'd been mistaken. *Now, she was turned on.*

She got to her feet slowly and turned her back to him. "I need help with the zip." She didn't actually, she could have dragged the dress over her head as she had this morning, but that didn't seem appropriate for this moment. She stood for a few seconds, and the horrible thought struck her that he might not get up and help. It melted away the instant she felt him lift the weight of her hair over one shoulder to expose the zip. His fingers brushed hot against her neck, and it took all of her efforts not to turn around. The sound of the zipper sliding down was indecent in the quiet room. Sophie couldn't be certain, but she thought he ran the lightest of fingertips down her spine as he went.

"Take it off," he breathed against her ear, then slid back into his chair to watch her again, his long legs sprawled out in front of him.

Sophie turned to face him, and the raw lust in his eyes was so unfamiliar, so powerful, that she couldn't tear her eyes away. She slipped the dress off one shoulder and then the other, then held her breath as she let go of the material and allowed it to slither to the floor.

Lucien's eyes moved slowly from hers, over her shoulders, and lingered on her breasts encased in black silk. Sophie squirmed, and fought the urge to bring her hands up to cover herself.

"Stand still."

He leaned in, poured the champagne and handed her a glass. She took it and drank deeply, letting the bubbles fizz on her tongue.

His eyes moved from her breasts to her stomach, lower to her black silk knickers.

"Turn around."

Fuck. Sophie wanted to gather up her clothes and run. Or… maybe she didn't. She found that she wanted to turn around and let him stare at her backside.

She turned around.

For endless, silent seconds, he didn't move a muscle. Sophie rubbed a finger up and down the stem of her glass as she wondered what he was thinking. She badly wanted to see his face. She knocked back half of her champagne, terrified that her silk-clad backside didn't meet his approval.

She never usually wore stockings. It had taken ten minutes this morning to find the hold-ups in the back of her wardrobe, but she was glad of the effort now.

She was on the verge of turning round when she felt Lucien's hand on her waist. Sophie drew in a sharp breath and arched her back as his warm hand slid around her to splay over her rib cage.

His other hand took her champagne glass and placed it on the table. He was so close behind her that she could feel the heat of him. When he stepped closer still, hard against her from shoulder to hip, his hands swept up and covered her breasts. Sophie heard him make a sound low in his throat, and then he turned her around in his arms to face him.

God, he was tall. She looked up into his face, and his hand slid down her spine to caress her backside. He wound her hair around his other hand, all the way up her back until he had it tight enough in his fist to tip her chin up. His fingers bit into the cheek of her bottom, right along the silken edge of her knickers. Dan was always gentle, and at that moment Lucien was anything but. He was raw, and strong, and Sophie wanted him more than she'd ever wanted anyone else in her life.

How could she be here, half naked in his arms without having even so much as kissed him?

She slid her hands up onto the wall of his chest and touched him for the first time. Her hands registered hard heat, and even through his shirt she could feel the steady beat of his heart.

"Unbutton it."

Oh, yes please. Sophie worked the buttons open and slid the material back over his shoulders, and he yanked it off his arms and threw it to the floor.

Up close and bare-chested, Lucien was heart-stoppingly fabulous. The soft silk of her bra brushed against the hardness of his chest, and Sophie melted into him.

Lucien's breathing was audible but steady as he caught hold of her hands. He snagged them both behind her back in one of his own larger ones, and his other hand slid around the nape of her neck to draw her mouth to his.

She was captive, at his mercy, and she loved it.

"Beautiful Sophie," he murmured against her lips, and then, at last, he lowered his head and kissed her.

Sophie's senses reeled at the first touch of his mouth on hers, soft and then hard and so filled with sexual intent that she trembled. He bit her lips and then licked them better. Explored her mouth with his hot, potent tongue as his firm hand cupped the back of her head. Being kissed by Lucien made Sophie feel as if everyone who'd kissed her before should queue up for lessons from him. Her knees buckled, but he had her so securely in his grip that it didn't even matter.

"Easy," he murmured into her mouth.

His hand slid around her throat, and then down to trace across the silk-encased curves of her breasts. Sophie arched against him, desperate for more, and she groaned as his erection pressed hard into her stomach.

He lifted his head to look down into her face, then eased his knee between her legs.

"You have no idea how many ways I'm going to make you come."

Sophie all but yelped. He was filthy, and she couldn't get enough of him. She was desperate to touch him, but he gripped her hands a fraction tighter when she wriggled in an attempt to free them.

Lucien shook his head. "Not yet, Princess." He slid his thigh further between her legs. Delicious friction. With his free hand he pulled her bra straps down to bare her breasts to his eyes.

Sophie gasped and felt her nipples stiffen as she watched him lean his head slightly to one side and stare openly at her body. He rocked his erection harder against her and licked his lips as his ragged breathing belied his apparent cool control. He was every bit as excited as she was.

"So pink." Lucien bent to suckle each of her nipples in turn, drawing a splutter of desire from Sophie's throat. She wanted to push her hands into his hair and hold him there, but he wouldn't release her wrists. Instead, he started to rock her on his thigh. The silk of her knickers rubbed her sex. Backwards. Forwards. Backwards. Forwards. Harder, until she rode him like a lap dancer on a pole, shameless in her need for him to finish what he'd started between her legs.

"That's better," he crooned, kissing her throat when she let her head fall backwards. "Let it go." He played with her breasts, watching her face for reactions. Stroking. Cupping. Rolling her nipples hard enough to send answering shots of desire firing through her body.

"Lucien…" she breathed his name. "Lucien…"

He arched an eyebrow as his fingers trailed down the soft curve of her stomach, every touch like a million tiny electric volts.

A crooked half smile crossed his lips as she bucked against him. He leaned in and kissed her ear. "Tell me what you want me to do, Sophie." His fingers stroked the along the edge of her knickers, making her stomach muscles jump in response. "I won't do it unless you ask me to." He licked the hollow at the base of her throat.

She knew exactly what she wanted.

"Lucien, please… touch me."

His answering laugh was pure filth. "Not nearly good enough, Ms. Black." He cupped one of her breasts in his hands and bent his head. "You have perfect tits." He licked her nipple and flicked his eyes upwards to her face. Sophie watched his tongue slide over the pink nub, mesmerised by what he was doing to her. Her breasts throbbed, and she ached between her legs for him. "Is this what you want, Sophie?"

He slipped his fingers inside her knickers and cupped her.

Sophie writhed with pleasure. "God, yes. Yes…" she moaned and pushed herself down into his hand.

Lucien straightened and clamped her, vice-like, against him, his hand down her knickers and his tongue in her mouth.

"Tell me exactly what you want me to do. Say the words."

Sophie had never known lust like it. She was so close to coming, and Lucien must know it. She eased her legs further apart and rubbed herself against his fingers. "Open me," she whispered, and instantly his fingers parted her. Sophie could feel his warm, strong fingers hovering, ready for orders.

"Touch my clit," she breathed. Lucien looked at her, an expression of lazy triumph alight in his eyes.

"Like this, Princess?" He started to stroke her, drawing slow circles on her clitoris with his thumb.

Sophie shuddered exquisitely and closed her eyes as the delicious sensations spiralled up through her body. His tongue explored her mouth, his skilled fingers more insistent than ever between her legs.

"God, Lucien…" Sophie arched, so close to climax that the only thought in her mind was release. His fingers slid down to her opening, and he rubbed his thumb over her mouth. "Come on Sophie, ask for more."

"Put your fingers inside me," she whispered, her heart banging and her desire ratcheting tighter.

Lucien made a guttural sound and moved her forwards on his thigh, then pushed two fingers all the way inside her. Sophie cried out at the intimacy, and Lucien's mouth softened over hers to an ultra-gentle kiss.

He stroked her clitoris with his thumb, crooking his fingers inside her, and Sophie lost hold of the threads on her control. She felt her climax begin at his fingertips, and Lucien's other hand tightened around her wrists to hold her up when her legs went from beneath her. He kissed her through it as her body stiffened, and thrust his fingers deeper into her when she bucked hard against his hand.

"That's it, Princess," he whispered. "I can feel you coming." His fingers were inside her to the knuckle, his thumb quickening on her clitoris.

"Christ, I can't wait to fuck you," he muttered, then thrust again. And again. And again, until Sophie lost it completely. She had nowhere to go besides over the top... she cried out and tossed her head back in wild, liberated abandon. Lucien's admiration made her powerful, sexy and uninhibited. She'd never known an orgasm like it, and she was greedy for more, more, more. He'd unleashed something new within her, a raw sexual need that had for too long been buried beneath the detritus of everyday life. Beneath the detritus of her broken marriage. Sophie couldn't bring herself to feel guilty. *Not yet.* Not with Lucien's fingers still moving lazily inside her, and his slow, tantalising kiss still on her lips, as he released her hands.
He'd shown her how sex was supposed be, and there was no going back.

Chapter Seven

As the glow of her orgasm wore off, Sophie slid slowly back to reality. She couldn't believe she'd been so brazen. *Or so unfaithful.* She wriggled out of Lucien's arms and sat down in the chair behind her, pulling her underwear back into place and holding her suddenly hot face in her hands.

What was she doing? She was in a sex club for God's sake, and had just allowed her boss bring her to orgasm. Or to be more accurate, she'd begged him to.

Who was she? And oh, God. Dan.

Lucien sprawled back in the chair opposite and propped his feet up on the coffee table, still shirtless, still sexy as sin. He crossed his arms over his chest.

"Sophie. Look at me."

She couldn't. She was mortified.

"Look. At. Me."

There was no ignoring him. She dropped her hands and met his eyes. How could he look so entirely relaxed, lounging as if he didn't have a care in the world? Well, maybe he didn't, but she did.

"I'm a married woman, Lucien."

"Yes. And your husband is screwing someone else, so the way I see it, this makes you square."

Sophie shook her head. "This isn't a game of tit for tat, Lucien, it's my marriage. I've loved Dan since I was seventeen years old."

Tears welled in her eyes and she dashed at them with the back of her hand. She'd always thought that she and Dan were the real deal. When the cracks had started to appear, she'd frantically papered over them, had made excuses to herself for him. It was agony to rip through the brittle wrapping and expose the ugly truth beneath.

"Christ, Lucien." Her heart ached. "What if I'm wrong? What if he isn't even having an affair?"

Lucien fixed his gaze on the window, suddenly expressionless.

"You seemed pretty certain."

Sophie shrugged and reached for her dress.

"Did I? Maybe I was just telling myself that because it was convenient, because I wanted to give myself permission to… to screw you." She made herself say the word.

"You haven't screwed me," he said. "Yet."

"Yet?" She shook her head to try and clear it. "Lucien, I need to go."

"No, you don't. Be brave, Sophie. Stay here."

She stood up to step into her dress, but he stood too and caught hold of her shoulders. When she looked up his face was deadly serious.

"This isn't about your husband, Sophie. It's about you. It's about the fact that you're a young woman trapped in an unfaithful marriage." His hands moved up to cradle her face, his thumbs warm along her jawbone.

"Christ Almighty. How can he lie next to you and not want you?"

Tears scorched Sophie's throat again, and she swallowed them down.

Jesus. Lucien was dangerous enough when he was being his usual cocky self, but like this? Perceptive and raw? He was lethal.

Lucien took the dress from her hands and threw it on the chair behind him. "Don't lie to yourself because you feel guilty, Sophie. He's cheating, and you deserve better. You deserve to be adored, and you deserve to be fucked until you can't stand up."

Sophie stared at him and her insides twisted with desire. That was just about the sexiest thing anyone had ever said to her, and the way he was gazing at her now with undisguised carnality was just about the sexiest way anyone had ever looked at her, too.

She'd never known anyone like Lucien, so in touch with their own sensuality, so unencumbered by unnecessary inhibition.

He must have sensed that his words had found a crack in her armour, because he moved in close and took her hand.

"Come with me. I want you to see something." He led her across the room to the huge, gilt-framed, floor-standing mirror. "Look in the mirror, Sophie."

She tried to pull away but he held her firm. "Look. Tell me what you see."

She looked, reluctantly. And she saw the same person she always saw reflected back at her. The same yet subtly different. More grown-up? More knowing?

Black silk underwear, hold-ups, high heels. Long, tumbled blonde hair. A kiss-swollen mouth, and the liquid, sensual eyes of a satisfied woman.

And standing behind her, a head and shoulders taller, Lucien. Shirtless.

Beautiful.

Her Viking warrior, and now her Viking lover.

"Let me tell you what I see." Lucien said, his hands on her shoulders.

"I see a woman with the face of an angel." He ran the back of his fingers down her cheek. "A face that makes men want to fuck her just to see how she looks when she comes."

Sophie stared at him in the mirror, shocked and mesmerised.

"She has the kind of curves that make men want to touch her."

He splayed a big warm hand over her pale stomach, making her skin tauten and her breath catch in her throat.

"I see a woman who deserves to be treated like a princess."

He only had to touch her and it was as if he'd flicked the 'seduce me now' switch in her head.

"Look at you, Sophie." He was so close that she could feel the warmth of his breath tickle her neck. "You're like a peach waiting to be plucked from the tree." He stepped flush against her, her back against his chest.

"Velvet soft skin." He trailed his fingertips down her arms.

"Luscious curves." He covered her breasts with his hands and stroked them through her bra.

"Ripe." He slid a hand between her legs and cradled her. Sophie watched his every move in the mirror with wide eyes, almost too turned on to breathe.

"Juicy." He groaned as he slid his hand inside her knickers. "So fucking juicy." He moved his fingers along her sex, still wet from the first time he'd made her come.

"I want to lick your juices, Sophie."

Sophie could feel his erection pressing hard into her back, and all she could think of was how much she wanted him to carry on making her feel this good. The sight of them in the mirror was like a life size soft porn movie; she couldn't take her eyes away from his hand moving inside her knickers.

"Tell me that isn't beautiful," he said against her ear.

She couldn't. The fact was that he made her beautiful.

"Stay there." Sophie almost cried out in protest when he eased his hands off her and backed away. He returned moments later with her glass of champagne in one hand, and a large, silver vibrator in the other.

Sophie gaped. Whatever she'd been expecting, it wasn't that.

"Which one would you like first?" he asked, that lazy, cock-sure smile back in place.

"Lucien, no. I don't want to…"

"Sophie, Sophie, Sophie." He handed her the champagne and shook his head. "Don't tell me you don't want this. I saw you in my office, the way thinking about that toy turned you on."

"But I've never…" she eyed the vibrator with apprehension. "I've never really used anything like… like that…" she tailed off, flame-cheeked, and swallowed a huge mouthful of champagne. "It's just not my thing."

He laughed and came to stand behind her again. "That's just

the thing, Princess. I don't think you know what your *thing* is." His arm slipped around her waist, the silver vibrator in his hand. He flicked the switch and it hummed quietly into life.

Sophie stood stock still, knowing full well that she wasn't going to stop him. Right now, he could do just about anything he wanted.

"You've lived your safe, vanilla existence." He touched the tip of the vibrator between the swell of her breasts, and unclipped her bra at the same time in one swift movement. She gasped and went to hold onto it, but he was too quick and whipped it out of her hands.

"Stop hiding from me." He moved her hair behind her shoulders to fully expose her naked breasts. "Look at you." His eyes darkened with lust and he ran the head of the vibrator up her stomach. "You're wasted on the occasional bout of missionary sex with a disinterested man." He placed the tip of the vibrator against one of her nipples, and Sophie's eyes widened at the new sensation. Lucien's teeth grazed her neck as he moved the vibrator around her other nipple. *Jesus.* Sophie felt the erotic vibrations fizz from her pebble hard nipples to her groin, and she arched into the erotic waves of pleasure that lapped through her.

"I see you. *Really* see you," he whispered, watching her eyes in the mirror. "I see the girl in there who's greedy for more."

He slid the vibrator down her body and nuzzled it in between her legs. "Are you still sure this isn't your thing, Sophie?"

She shook her head and leaned back against him, reaching an arm behind her head to hold onto his neck. She wasn't sure of anything apart from how damn good that vibrator felt as he ran it over the scant silk that covered her sex.

He moved his hands to hook his thumbs into the sides of her knickers as Sophie watched her bare, jutting breasts rise and fall in the mirror. He was going to strip her naked and fuck her with that big silver vibrator, and she couldn't wait.

"You want this." He eased her underwear down, then

straightened to look in her eyes again. She chewed her lip and nodded slowly.

"Look again. See what I see."

Sophie saw herself, naked apart from her hold-ups and high heels, and she'd never felt so profoundly sexy in her life.

"Kneel down." Her eyes jumped up to his in confusion. "Here, by the mirror."

He placed a hand on her shoulder and applied a little pressure to encourage her, and she dropped down uncertainly to kneel with her bottom resting on her ankles. Lucien looked massive standing behind her, and she could clearly see the swell of his erection close to her head. He looked like the world's sexiest cowboy: all brawn and bare chest with a vibrator in place of a gun.

He lowered himself and knelt behind her, bracketing her legs with his own, the silenced vibrator on the floor next to him. He wrapped his arms around her body and held her close, and those few unexpected moments of tenderness overwhelmed her. Lucien's arms were strong and warm, his lips gentle as they grazed her shoulder. Sophie looked at his bowed head, at the way he closed his eyes as he kissed her, and she melted for him again. Then he opened his eyes and gave her that crooked, sex god smile, and the moment was gone. Her pulse rocketed in erotic anticipation of what might happen next.

Lucien didn't keep her waiting to find out. He placed his hands on her knees and parted her legs, then kept his hands on her kneecaps to still her as she instinctively tried to close them again.

"Uh-uh. Open."

Panic spiralled in Sophie's belly. *Or was it excitement?* The two sensations had been intertwined in her guts from the moment she'd set foot across the threshold of Lucien's office and entered his presence. She wanted to close her legs, it was too lewd, both of them looking at her glistening sex in the mirror, but then… she didn't want to.

Lucien's hands moved along her inner thighs when he was

certain she wasn't going to clamp shut on him. His fingers traced the soft skin, and she moaned when he ran one finger down her core. Up again, ultra slow. Sophie's breath came in short gasps, and threatened to stop altogether when he moved his hands to cover her own and took them back down between her legs. His big warm hands over her smaller ones.

"Open yourself for me, Sophie." She squeezed her eyes tight, and he sank his teeth into her neck almost hard enough to make her cry out.

"Don't close your eyes. Watch." He moved her fingers with his own, guiding her actions, forcing her to expose her inner self to them both in the mirror. "You see? Can you see how fucking gorgeous you are?" He touched his index finger against her clitoris, and smiled at the way she jolted and moaned with pleasure. "That's better. Don't move your hands. Watch. Watch my fingers." She did as she was told, lost in the intensity of the feelings he'd unleashed. She wanted to come. She wanted them both to watch her come. *Yes. Yes. Don't stop.* She licked her lips, lost in the way his big brown fingers moved on her in just the right way. And then he stopped, and she gasped in frustration because she'd been so close, so very, very close. And then she gasped again, but this time in apprehension, because he'd turned the vibrator on and slid it down behind her back. It buzzed rudely against the fullness of her backside, and then Sophie's eyes widened as Lucien ran the tip between her legs. She could see its silver head throbbing, and she rocked her hips in an effort to move it closer to her clitoris.

"Greedy girl." Lucien pushed it forward to give her what she wanted for the briefest of seconds. Long enough to make her squirm, too brief to let her come. He was her heavenly torturer, running the buzzing tip up and down her sex, never letting her have what she needed.

"Do you want it inside your cunt, Sophie?" He let the very tip of the vibrator slide inside her.

"Yes," she breathed, horrified by the fact that his crude choice of words only excited her even more. "Yes." She was beyond desperate for him to fill her up.

"Princess," he murmured against her hair, and then he fed the throbbing vibrator all the way inside her in one long, languorous push. Sophie moaned with pleasure, unable to take her eyes off his hands as he worked the silver shaft into her. She started to shake, to physically tremble with bone-deep pleasure, and he kept her right on the edge of her climax, daring her with his eyes and his hands to go further for him than she ever had before.

"Yes…yes…" she moaned and he thrust the vibrator deep inside her to the hilt, then twisted it until the clit stimulator hit her sweet spot. He held it there.

"Fuck, yeah," he whispered. Look at you…" Her body started to jerk. "Watch yourself come, Sophie." He had her spread wide open and the stimulator held steady against her clitoris when she tried to squirm away from the intensity, making her convulse with the violence of her orgasm as it exploded through her. She could hear someone screaming with pleasure, and it took her several long moments to register the sound as her own. Her body had taken over control from her mind with an animal instinct that she was powerless to fight. Lucien Knight was feral, and she loved it.

Sophie slumped in Lucien's arms as he gathered her close to his chest. She needed to be still, to let her heart stop hammering and her body stop shaking.

What was she doing? Aftershocks of shame crept over her, and she closed her eyes against the image of herself naked in another man's arms. What had looked so erotic moments ago now looked shoddy.

What hold did this man have over her? He only had to touch her and common sense flew away, leaving her wanton and craving his touch. Even now, with the weight of shame on her shoulders, she couldn't see him as anything but beautiful. It wasn't his fault that her marriage was broken, and much as he might think so, letting herself be seduced wasn't the key to mending it.

Lucien stirred behind her, but her bones felt too heavy to lift from the floor. She needn't have worried. Moments later his strong arms slid beneath her and lifted her like a child, his chest warm against her cheek as he settled her against him. He crossed to the bed and laid her gently down, then tucked the covers around her lightly shivering body and smoothed her damp hair from her cheek.

If he'd been anything other than breathtakingly gentle, Sophie might have found the resolve to call a halt to it, but his tenderness unbuttoned her defenses. It stole away her shame and her anger, and left her with only a sense of inevitability and calm, and the weary ache of a satisfied lover. He stroked her hair, and soothed her with whispered, incomprehensible words. She strained to catch them, but they floated away from her on the coat tails of sleep. All except for one.
Princess.

Chapter Eight

Lucien sat in the chair beside the bed and watched Sophie sleep. She'd been out for the count for a couple of hours, and downstairs the club had come alive. He'd walked the floor beneath an hour back and found himself satisfied by the number of people flooding through the doors, every one of them bold-eyed and expectant. He loved their lack of inhibition, their courage to shun social boundaries and to be whoever the hell they wanted in this place that he'd created.

The Gateway Club was precisely what it said above the door. A gateway to sexual freedom for anyone brave enough to enter.

He looked back at Sophie again. She'd frustrated the hell out of him from the moment she'd sashayed into his office in heels she could barely stand up in, and she'd stunned him when she'd turned around and forced words out of her mouth that clearly mortified her. Her embarrassment had lost the battle with her pluck, and it impressed him. The girl was eighty percent kitten and twenty percent lioness, and he considered it his mission to make her roar. Sexual potential shone out of her like a beacon, and her insistence otherwise only made him want to prove her wrong even more.

Besides, there was the small matter of her husband. If there was one thing that really made Lucien's skin crawl, it was men who treated women badly. His investigator had dug around and turned up evidence to prove that Dan's other woman had been a permanent fixture in Sophie's marriage for some considerable time.

How could the man do it? How could he tell barefaced lies to the woman he professed to love?

Darkness settled over Lucien's heart as long-buried memories of his mother's heartache swam through his head. Her only crime had been to love his father too much, and she'd died for her cause. Alone, save for a bottle of pills and a scrunched up photograph of her husband. She'd lived her life in the shadows of Lucien's father's deception, and for the most part she'd conned herself that she was happy. Right up until the day she couldn't ignore it any more because it was shoved rudely in her face when she'd visited him at work and found him astride his secretary on the desk.

She'd been faced with the truth in all its ugliness, and it had broken her.

Lucien had been too young back then to save his mother, but he was going to make damn sure that Sophie didn't get sucked down into that same cycle of destruction. She was teetering right on the verge of confronting her husband, and Lucien intended to tool her up for the fight.

In a small hotel room in Crete, Dan slumped in a similar chair next to a similar bed and watched another woman sleeping. *What was he doing?* This was the first time he'd spent more than twenty-four solid hours in Maria's company, and the reality of being with someone other than Sophie around the clock had hit home hard. Meetings with Maria for clandestine dinners and afternoon sex sessions had become pleasurable fixtures in his life over the last eighteen months. From the moment they'd met at a work party, she'd made no secret of the fact that she fancied him. She was flirty. Sexy. She was fun, and she didn't care if he forgot to put the bins out or left his washing on the bedroom floor. She was exciting in her unfamiliarity, and she wanted him. It took no effort at all to separate her in his mind from his marriage vows.

If anything, he told himself, screwing Maria helped his marriage. Maria did things that Sophie wouldn't dare. He was a satisfied man, and in every other area than the bedroom his relationship with Sophie was ideal.

He'd compartmentalised his life in his head perfectly.

Sophie, his wife and best friend. Maria, his twice a week lover.

It had been the ideal set up, until now.

Until this week.

Maria had been making noises about getting away together for months but he'd managed to dodge it. She knew his situation. He was a married man. But then events had conspired against him, and he'd found himself unable to get out of it this time. Maria hadn't exactly said that she'd tell Sophie about their affair, but she'd intimated as much, and the threat alone was enough to have him packing his suitcase and telling his biggest lie yet.

Maria had met him at the airport, and from there on in, he'd known with utter conviction that it was wrong. He didn't want to browse duty free with her, because buying Sophie a new bottle of scent was part of their usual holiday ritual. Being with Maria twenty-four seven had highlighted all of the differences between the two women in his life that he'd never taken the time to think about. Sure, Maria might not grumble about bins or dirty washing as yet, but the minutiae of temporarily living with her had exposed their incompatibilities more than their strengths. Or maybe he was being unfair. It probably shouldn't matter that Maria slept on the wrong side of the bed, or that she preferred tea to coffee in the morning. It really shouldn't faze him that she was the sightseeing type rather than a bake on the beach girl, or that she had no clue how to play poker on the balcony late at night.

But the fact was, all these things *did* bother him, because they rammed home the fact that she just wasn't Sophie. She wasn't the woman he loved, the woman who knew him inside out.

Did Sophie know about Maria? How could she not?

Christ, he hoped not.

He dropped his head in his hands, feeling trapped. He wanted to go home.

Chapter Nine

Sophie opened her eyes. Warm, subdued lamps lit the room, and she was incredibly comfortable. Fragment by fragment, the memory of the past few hours clicked back into place as she woke, and a glance under the covers confirmed her fears. She was naked. She hadn't dreamt it. She really had let Lucien do those things to her.

Where was he? She sat up in bed, the sheet clutched against her nude body. He must have heard her movements, because a second later he appeared in the doorway.

"I'll take it as a compliment that you slept so well." He leaned against the doorframe with his arms folded across his chest. Sophie frowned, wrong-footed by the fact that he'd changed his clothes. She hadn't seen him in anything other than business dress, but right now, in soft, battered jeans and a faded black t-shirt that clung to his well-defined body, he was a brand new kind of gorgeous.

"What time is it?" she asked, disorientated by the darkness and Lucien's nearness.

"Almost midnight."

Sophie squinted at him. She'd been asleep for more than three hours. *Oh God.* She was in a sex club. Heaven only knew what was happening beneath her.

"Lucien. This is wrong. I shouldn't be here." Her voice came out hoarser than she'd expected.

He shook his head and disappeared for a few seconds, then returned with a tray. He placed it down on the bed next to her, then sat down alongside it.

"Eat. You must be hungry."

Sophie glanced down at the array of food. Delicate sandwiches. Bowls of fruit. Chocolate truffles.

She looked up at Lucien again, wondering how he could expect her to sit there naked and snack. She was his PA. He was her boss.

"Is this how you welcome all new staff, Lucien? A trip to a sex club, a quick fumble, and a sandwich? It's not very classy."

She'd aimed to offend, but he just laughed off her rudeness.

"That wasn't a fumble, Sophie. It was a prelude."

She'd been half-considering eating a sandwich, but the idea lost its appeal at his words. "A prelude?"

He nodded and helped himself to a cherry from the bowl.

"A prelude." He sank his teeth into the dark, glossy skin of the cherry and ripped the flesh from the stone.

There was always an element of surprise in conversations with Lucien; he was as unpredictable as quicksilver. Sophie watched him in silence and waited for more.

"I have a proposition for you." He reached for another cherry.

Sophie shook her head. Where had her reality gone? She suddenly understood how Alice had felt when she'd tumbled down that rabbit hole. Had someone plucked her out of her own life and dropped her into a fantasy? She was naked in a sex club watching a Viking warrior suck on a cherry. This was not her average Tuesday evening. She couldn't speak. She didn't know any appropriate words.

"Stay with me this week."

Whoa. She knew the answer to that one.

"What? No!" He might be gorgeous, but he was clearly crazy.

"Give me one good reason why not," he said, then stretched out next to her on the bed and dangled another indecently big cherry over his mouth by the stalk.

"Because... because I don't want to, for one thing."

"Of course you do, you're just afraid to admit it." Lucien

laughed and bit the cherry in half. "A better reason, please."

Sophie shook her head. "You are the cockiest man I've ever met."

"Yada yada yada." He gestured for her to move on, and she stared at him, frustrated. She was trapped. Her clothes were strewn across the other side of the room, and the sheet was pinned beneath his body. Short of treating him to a strip show there was no getting away from this conversation, and he knew it perfectly well.

He turned big, innocent blue eyes on her. "Do you have a cat? Is that it? Is Mr. Tibbles going to die without you going home to feed him?"

She narrowed her eyes and looked away. "I don't have a cat."

"A dog, then? Two screaming kids?"

Sophie sighed and flopped back on the pillow, the sheet clutched under her arms. "It's just me and Dan."

"Who isn't there." The quiet starkness of his words stripped away Sophie's anger and left her defenseless.

"Right. Let's start this conversation again. Stay with me until Sunday."

Sophie propped herself up on one elbow and turned to him. "What for?"

His eyes slid to hers. "Because you owe it to yourself. Because you're young, and beautiful, and there is so much more to sex than you've experienced so far. You deserve to know it all, to feel it all, and I want to be the one to show you."

"Has it occurred to you that I might not want to know?"

He shook his head with a low, sexy laugh. "It's occurred to me that you think you don't want to know. But then I touch you, and you come alive." He reached across and picked a peach from the tray. "Aren't you curious, Sophie? *Really*, don't you want to know?"

Convention decreed that Sophie should refuse, but his directness demanded the same candour from her. She couldn't bring herself to lie, yet equally couldn't allow herself to admit the truth.

Lucien turned the peach over in his hands, knowing full well that it was so much more than an innocent piece of fruit.

He trailed a fingertip down the curve of it, and he may as well have been stroking her bottom. He was doing it again, subtly infiltrating her thoughts. If he ever gave up his life as the king of a sex empire, he'd make a crack hot hypnotist.

"Stay because I want you to, Sophie." He brought the peach up to his nose and inhaled deeply.

"Stay because I can make you feel better than anyone else ever has." He put the peach to his mouth, closed his eyes, and sank his teeth in deep.

Sophie's nipples stiffened beneath the sheet. She couldn't deny it. He'd won. She wanted his mouth on her rather than that peach, but the words wouldn't come out.

He propped himself up on his elbow, mirroring her pose, then offered the peach up to her lips, close enough for her to taste it. "Bite."

She closed her eyes and obeyed his command.

"It tastes like you." His words caressed her as she ate the soft flesh. "Sweet." His fingers touched her mouth as she swallowed. "And tempting." Sophie couldn't stop herself. She opened her mouth and sucked his finger in, swirling the sweet peach juices around him with her tongue. When she opened her eyes, he slid his finger slowly out of her mouth and into his own.

"I like the taste of you," he said. "Tell me you'll stay."

Sophie gave him the tiniest of nods. "I'll stay," she whispered, then cleared her throat. "I'll stay," she repeated, louder this time. "I want to stay with you, Lucien."

Lucien's answering smile was full of sexual promise, and in one swift movement he leaned over and rolled Sophie on top of him. He was fully clothed, and there were layers of bedding between them, but Sophie could still clearly feel his arousal pressing up into her stomach.

His hands swept down the length of her exposed spine,

making her gasp. She was nude apart from her hold-up stockings, and Lucien wasted no time in helping himself.

He filled his hands with her backside. "Now that's peachy," he said, with a sidelong glance at the abandoned plate of fruit, then he snaked a hand around the back of her neck to pull her mouth down onto his kiss. Fireworks exploded in her gut as his tongue slid over hers and his hips rocked, hard into softness. She couldn't help it, she opened her legs a little for him, and his fingers slid into the crevices of her backside. His other hand moved to cup her head against his.

His fingers moved in long strokes, touching her everywhere. Sliding just inside her, then back out to trace lazy figures of eight on her clitoris.

"I'm going to lick you here."

Sophie groaned with anticipation. *God, she wanted his tongue there.*

"And here." He slid his fingers inside her again for a second, then slipped them out again and around to caress her bottom.

"And here." His finger stroked the tight little entrance, making her squirm with shock.

"Lucien! No."

He sunk his teeth into her lower lip. "No?"

He didn't move his fingers away from her bottom, but his touch was so feather-gentle that she stopped trying to wriggle away. "It might surprise you."

She shook her head. It was a taboo that she'd never been interested in breaking. And she still wasn't, but there was something undeniably sexy at the feel of Lucien touching her there.

"I'll add it to my list," he breathed into her mouth.

Sophie lifted her head a fraction, and the movement pushed her spine downwards, which in turn pushed her backside down a little deeper onto his hand. Her eyes opened wider. He said nothing, but instead gave her a long, knowing look. He was on to her. He knew that she'd already grown to like the alien feeling of his attention there.

"What list?"

"The one in my head of things I'm going to make you do this week, Princess."

Sophie felt beyond filthy. She was lying on top of a man who was playing with her bottom and filling her ears with promises of a week of unadulterated, uncensored pleasure. She was full to the brim with dark, luscious desire, and ready to follow this big Viking sex god into his thrilling, unfamiliar world.

His hand lingered for another moment on her backside, then he sat up and rolled her off him.

"Get dressed, Sophie. We're going downstairs.

Chapter Ten

Sophie hung back by the open door to Lucien's suite, dressed once again in her green dress and high heels, but bereft of her knickers. They were in Lucien's pocket, and no amount of pleading for them back had made the slightest jot of difference. He'd laughed at the idea that she'd never before left the house without underwear, and pocketed them regardless of her protest.

He stood at the bottom of the small flight of stairs and beckoned to her.

"Come on, Sophie. I'm going to do a full walk through, and you're coming with me."

"But…" she glanced desperately down at his pocket. She really wanted the security of her knickers.

"Stop looking at my crotch and come here." He reached for her hand, taking the edge off his words. She stepped uncertainly down to stand next to him, feeling wrong and exposed even though she looked perfectly decent to the unknowing eye.

"That's better, Sophie. Now, I'm going to do a full check on the place, and you are going to do your job as my PA and accompany me."

Sophie found small solace in the fact that he'd given the event a work-related slant.

"Shouldn't I have a clipboard, or something?" she asked. She'd feel so much better if she looked official, distinct from the rest of the club's clientele. Something to mark her out as staff, rather than as a pleasure-seeker.

Lucien laughed at her.

"Don't be ridiculous. We're aiming to blend in, not stick out and put people off their…" he turned to her and licked his lips. "Their stride." He ran a hand over her backside and leaned close to her ear.

"I don't think I'm going to let you wear knickers again this week."

The man was lethal. This was all a big game to him, and he was a world-class player. Sophie straightened her spine and pushed her shoulders back. The thought of seeing the club with people in those rooms, on those beds… she shivered. She sort of wanted to run home, even without her knickers, but she had to acknowledge that a bigger part of her wanted to stay and see what lay beyond. She reminded herself that regardless of everything else, she was supposed to be here in her capacity as Lucien's PA. If she thought of it that way, maybe she could make it through the next few hours.

"Lead the way, Mr. Knight."

He inclined his head and placed his hand on the small of her back.

"Stay close to me. No one will touch you unless you touch them first."

She'd been apprehensive before. She was terrified now. *What if she stumbled into someone, or brushed past them by mistake?* Would they tie her to the bed and give her thirty lashes? And would Lucien intervene, or would he consider it all part of her sexual liberation?

"Sophie?" Lucien came to a stop and looked down at her. "For God's sake, just relax, will you? This way." He moved towards a fire exit, and threw her an enquiring look when she didn't automatically follow.

"We'll go down this way and come in through reception," he explained, holding out his hand again. "I want to see it through the eyes of our paying customers."

Sophie threw one last, longing glance over her shoulder at the now locked door that stood between her and sanctuary, and then followed Lucien out onto the fire escape.

Sophie clamped herself against Lucien's side as they bypassed the small queue at the front door. The club looked different now that darkness had descended. The smoked glass exterior took on a menacing stance without the sun to glint off it, and the subdued lighting in reception added to the air of anticipation that radiated from the waiting customers. Sophie sneaked the smallest glance at them as she passed, then looked away hastily. From what she could see, most people looked pretty regular. Maybe she'd overblown things in her mind. It was a club. She'd been clubbing enough times, the people in the queue had been no less dressed than regular clubbers.

Lucien nodded at the security staff and placed his hand on Sophie's back again to steer her past reception and through the double entrance doors.

He leaned down and placed his mouth close to her ear as they stepped down into the packed, shadowy club.

"We're not in Kansas anymore, Dorothy." The unexpectedness of the phrase made her suppress a giggle. She relaxed a little. Sophie let her eyes rove around, taking in the fact that this previously empty room was now filled with people. On first glimpse, it almost looked like any other club. Music pumped, the bar glittered with countless spirit and mixer bottles, and the dance floor heaved with gyrating people. However, a closer look confirmed that they weren't dressed like the clubbers outside. Obviously the changing rooms were mostly a place to get rid of eighty percent of your clothing. Women shimmered in tiny, see-through dresses, or basques, and occasionally next to nothing at all.

"Drink?" Lucien asked, raising his voice over the music. Sophie frowned.

"It doesn't seem very professional."

"Consider it part of your disguise."

He guided her to the bar, and Sophie's eyes wandered as Lucien ordered drinks from the immediately attentive barman. A guy was perched on a stool at the end of the bar, and it took several seconds for it to register with Sophie that his cock was buried in the mouth of the brunette between his knees. Holy fuck. She looked away hurriedly and found Lucien's amused blue eyes watching her. The subdued lighting shadowed his face and gave him a slightly menacing air. *Could she trust him to take care of her here?* What if he suddenly stripped his clothes off and expected her to jump naked into the writhing hot tub? It was strange. She'd only known him for a tiny amount of time, yet she was – unfathomably – certain that she could trust him.

He offered her one of two tumblers.

"What is it?"

"Vodka."

"Neat vodka?"

He shrugged. "You can have ice if you like."

She sipped it cautiously and straight away choked on the throat-stripping intensity of the spirit. Lucien rolled his eyes and held out her glass to the barman, who emptied a silver shovel of ice into it without a flicker of expression.

Lucien turned to lean against the bar and surveyed the room.

"Sit for a second. I need to watch it all working."

Sophie glanced down at the high designer metal stool next to him and wished she had some hand sanitiser.

"Just sit on it. It's scrupulously clean." Lucien anticipated her thoughts once again, and it was her turn to roll her eyes as she climbed up onto it. *Why did they make these things so bloody awkward?*

Lucien steadied the stool with his hand. "I wish I'd been standing in front of you just then. I think you just flashed that guy over there."

Sophie's eyes shot around in panic. There was no one watching her except for Lucien, who was openly laughing. He patted her knickers in his pocket.

"Funny," she muttered sourly, and crossed her legs to be doubly sure that no one could see up her skirt.

A woman with long black curls and a sprayed on red lace dress sashayed up to the bar next to Lucien, close enough to make ignoring her impossible. Her curvy body brushed against his from shoulder to thigh, and fear prickled along Sophie's skin. Had she got him wrong? Would he accept this woman's none-too-subtle invitation? Sophie glanced up at him as he inclined his head at the woman in impersonal greeting, then turned his back on her to face Sophie with deliberate slowness. The unexpectedness of his mouth on hers a second or two later knocked the breath from Sophie's lungs. He tasted of vodka and lust, and she opened her mouth to let his tongue glide over hers. His lips were firm, his hands even firmer as they held her hips.

"Was that another part of the disguise?" she breathed when he released her, her mouth tingling from the vodka and his kiss.

"No." His thumbs massaged her hipbones. "I kissed you because, even though you're totally overdressed, you're still the sexiest woman in the room."

He had a way of saying the last thing Sophie expected, of mixing up the tender with the filthy that rendered her speechless.

Even here in the middle of this charged, sexual atmosphere, Lucien shone. A carnal beacon. Dangerous. *Delicious.*

"Let's walk." He helped her down from the stool and led her around the edge of the dance floor. Sophie tried not to look too closely at people as she passed, but she couldn't stop her eyes from straying, or her body from reacting to it.

A woman wearing a tiny black thong hung upside down on the pole, a guy's hand between her spread legs. On the sofas, couples groped each other openly. Lucien's fingers laced through Sophie's and she held on tight when they passed a couple screwing against the wall, his trousers around his ankles, her legs wrapped around his hips. Lucien's arm fell around Sophie's waist. Reassuring. Predatory.

"This way."

He headed through an archway at the rear to somewhere he hadn't shown her on the earlier, tamer tour.

"Do you like the movies?" he whispered, and pulled her sideways into a darkened room.

It took a few seconds for Sophie's eyes to adjust to the darkness and realise she was inside a cinema, but not any kind of cinema she'd ever been to. Something told her that they wouldn't be buying popcorn here. The seats were all grouped in pairs and covered in leopardskin, and the movie scrolling across the screen was hardcore porn. Sophie stared at it, transfixed. She'd never really been attracted to any kind of porn, so to see it suddenly so lewd and huge in front of her came as a shock. There didn't seem to be all that many people in the room, but those that were there made no secret of the fact that they were having sex.

Lucien tugged her into a love chair tucked away right at the back of the room.

"Lucien, we can't…"

"It's marked private. No one will look unless invited."

His mouth landed on hers the instant he had her cornered, and the fire in her belly lit with indecent speed. She was surrounded by wall-to-wall sex, and in the arms of a man who wanted her with a passion that bordered on obsession. His lips clashed with hers, and his tongue thrashed and licked inside her mouth as his fingers sought her nipples through the material of her dress.

Lust slayed her. Fast, hard need made her crawl over to straddle his lap. His erection burned between them as he dragged her skirt up roughly and pushed his hand between her legs. She cried out, and he clamped his other hand over her mouth.

"Don't make a sound."

He pushed his fingers inside her, and her face contorted with the effort of silencing her pleasure.

"People will consider it okay to come and watch if you make a racket," he whispered, taking his hand off her mouth. She nodded, wide-eyed, afraid he was going to stop, knowing he wasn't. Operating on instinct, she reached down and massaged his bulging erection, then popped the top button of his jeans. This was the third time he'd touched her intimately, and she wanted to even up the score. She wanted to feel his length in her hands, in her mouth, inside her body. He moaned and shifted underneath her.

"Not here, Princess." Sophie grumbled in frustration when he caught her wrist. "I want to hear you scream the first time I fuck you."

He pulled her own hand down between her legs and nipped her ear.

"Get yourself off." His fingers still pumped inside her, rhythmic and deep. Sophie could feel her clitoris under her fingers, and she couldn't resist the urge to do as she was told. He licked the fingers of his other hand and reached around her thigh to stroke her perineum. She tensed, knowing where he was heading.

"Behave yourself." Lucien laughed into her mouth. "I'm fucking you with my fingers. You're fingering your own clit. Now I'm going to touch your ass, and you're going to love it."

His wet fingers stroked their way up to play around her anus just like before as his fingers pumped harder into her sex. Sophie moaned. It was filthy erotic, and he bit her lip when she started to lose control of her ability to be silent. "You're so fucking sexy, Sophie,' he murmured. He knew how close she was and urged her on with whispered sex words and deeper thrusts of his fingers. Sophie sunk her nails into his shoulders and ground her teeth as her orgasm started to build. Lucien sensed it and pounded his fingers faster into her, dripping words in her ears that embarrassed her with their crudeness and pushed her climax further over the boundaries.

It wasn't lovemaking. It was pure fucking. Sophie stiffened, and Lucien pushed his tongue into her mouth at the same time as he crooked his finger gently into her bottom. Sophie arched violently, full in every orifice, and her entire body shook with the effort of controlling her urge to scream out in dark, sublime ecstasy as she came in his hands. It went on, and on… wave after wave… she ground down on him and held on through the storm.

"Aren't you glad you aren't wearing knickers now?" he whispered as she stilled. Sophie rested her forehead against his. *Yes. Yes, she was.* Lucien eased his fingers out of her and straightened her dress over her thighs gently and deliberately. A smile played at the corners of his mouth.

"Shame you didn't bring that clip board. We could have crossed 'make Sophie orgasm in a sex club,' off my list." Lucien raised his eyebrows at her. "Top of the class, Ms. Black. You're progressing nicely."

Sophie stood up and smoothed her dress down, unsteady on her high heels. On the huge screen in front of her, a guy had some naked woman bent double over the bonnet of his car, and the camera zoomed in on his cock buried deep between her legs. Sophie's sex still throbbed from her orgasm, and she glanced back at Lucien behind her. She wanted his cock inside her, wanted him to fill her just like that woman on the screen.

"Can we go back upstairs?" she whispered croakily, running her hand over his crotch.

A low laugh rumbled in his throat.

"Easy, Princess." He put his hand on her bottom to propel her out of the cinema.

Back in the club, Sophie followed close behind Lucien to the staircase at the side of the dance floor. She was aware of other women's eyes on him as he passed them, and a feather of pride danced down her spine.

Hands off, girls. This one's mine. For this week, anyway.

After what had just happened in the cinema, Sophie felt a strange thread of connection to these people, and the beginnings of understanding of why they were there.

It was oddly liberating, a sense of belonging.

Whoa! What was she thinking? She didn't belong with these people. *Did she?* Was Lucien right? Was there a degenerate sex goddess lurking beneath her innocent skin?

She was already sure of one thing. She couldn't go back to her barely -there, suburban sex life with Dan.

She physically pushed any thoughts of him out of her head. They hurt too much. He was somewhere else, probably screwing someone else at that very moment, and just for this week, she wasn't going to feel guilty about doing exactly the same thing.

Chapter Eleven

Lucien led Sophie through the club. Through rooms full of strangers fucking each other. Past the hot tub, a tangle of naked limbs, a nude blonde woman with three men on her. One behind her. One in front of her between her spread thighs. The third standing over her, his cock in her mouth. She caught Sophie's eye as they passed through, a silent but unmistakable invitation to join in that had Sophie hurriedly averting her gaze. She might have let Lucien touch her here, but she had no desire to let anyone else.

Upstairs, Lucien opened door after door, and a kaleidoscope of x-rated images burned themselves on Sophie's retinas. The music from downstairs was up here too, a low sexual pulse that underpinned the action. If downstairs had seemed lewd, up here was downright obscene. Couples. Threesomes. Orgies. Lucien opened the door to the room containing the bed Sophie had tested, and this time around it wasn't empty. Three naked women were twined around each other in a Sapphic triangle.

A redhead stood at the end of the bed watching proceedings, one spike-heeled foot propped up on the mattress to give the woman kneeling on the floor between her legs better access. Lucien's hand massaged Sophie's behind as she stood rooted to the spot. She could clearly see the woman's tongue working its magic between the other's legs... flicking her clitoris... unlike most of the women in the club, she wasn't fully shaved. A triangle of soft red curls covered her sex, and somehow rendered the oral act more intimate, like watching wild animals.

"Fucking beautiful, isn't it?" Lucien whispered, and he moved her hand behind her to cover his bulging erection. Sophie's throat was parched. She didn't want to be turned on by lesbians. She didn't want to enjoy the sensation of Lucien's cock in her hand while she watched some woman get off on another woman's face. She wanted to leave, but Lucien was behind her blocking the way, and the woman started to gyrate. She was going to come, right here in front of Sophie. She stepped backwards, but only succeeded in being closer against the hardness of Lucien's body.

"No running. Watch her come. Can you see how close she is, Sophie?" Lucien rocked his cock into her hand against her backside.

"See how pink she is. Christ…" Lucien whispered. "You're even more beautiful, Sophie."

The woman was really moaning now, and splayed herself even wider with her fingers. Sophie couldn't take her eyes off her glistening sex, her lips spread for that greedy mouth.

"So wet…" Lucien breathed. "Are you wet, too Sophie?"

Sophie clutched his cock harder. *Yes.*

"Imagine how you're going to feel when I lick your clitoris like that."

Sophie tensed, too lost in animalistic sensation to feel embarrassed. The woman's tongue dipped inside her lover.

"Imagine how it's going to feel…" he pushed himself hot and hard against her hand, "when I fuck you, Sophie."

The woman's hips bucked against her lover's face, and Lucien's teeth sank into Sophie's ear.

"Come on. Show's over."

"I guess we can cross 'make you watch a live lesbian sex show' off that list, too," Lucien said dryly, as he guided her along the corridor. Sophie couldn't look at him. Her head was spinning. Too many sexual images. Too many positions. Too many emotions she hadn't expected and didn't know how to handle. She was ashamed of her reaction back there in that room, embarrassed by the fact that she'd found it so erotic.

Lucien was pushing her too far. She had no clue who she was any more, how to act, how to return to normal after he'd done with her.

"Please, Lucien. Can we go back now?"

She turned to him, and his eyes scanned her face for a few silent seconds.

"Enough for now, huh?" He cupped her cheek.

"More than." Sophie said, her throat suddenly clogged with tears. This was all wrong, wrong, wrong.

"I want to go home." Sophie gathered her bag from Lucien's bedroom as soon as they reached his suite. She was weary more than tired, jaded more than enlightened, and she wanted to be alone to keep her own counsel. Lucien seemed to rob her of the ability for rational thought; one touch and her resolve melted like an ice cube faced with a blowtorch. She didn't want to melt any more. If only she could stay cool and composed around him, then none of this would have happened.

Lucien put his head on one side.

"You could always sleep here."

Sophie shook her head and glanced away from him.

"I need to go home, Lucien." She knew her voice sounded watery, probably because she'd had to force it past the tears that welled up in her throat.

Lucien looked as if he was going to say something but then thought better of it. He reached for his keys off the desk and tossed them up in the air.

"That's all right." He caught his keys and nodded towards the door. "I'll drive you now."

Sophie puffed out hard, relieved that he'd chosen not to battle with her. "Thank you," she mumbled, following behind him as he locked the door and headed for the fire exit again. She gulped in lungfuls of cool night air as she clicked her way down the metal fire steps, beyond grateful that Lucien hadn't steered her back out through the club. She couldn't face all of that again tonight.

He blipped the car and she slid into the safety of the leather interior, the glass and metal around her a welcome wall separating her from the debauchery beyond.

And then Lucien was inside with her, the grandmaster of all of the debauchery, and she wasn't safe in the car, or anywhere. Because if Lucien was around, she wasn't safe from herself.

They drove in silence, the car eating up the miles like candy. Sophie's body ached, but her heart ached more. Everything was such a jumble in her head. She loved Dan. She wanted Lucien. Sex with Dan was… she squeezed her eyes together. *Sex with Dan was boring.* She just hadn't known it until Lucien had stripped the scales from her eyes. Jesus, she hadn't even had sex with Lucien, not properly, but he'd still excited her more in the last two days that Dan had in the last few years.

Her eyes slid to his profile as he watched the road, handling the sports car with easy expertise. Lights from street signs and shop fronts flashed multi- coloured shadows across the slopes and angles of his face. Neon greens, hot pinks, dangerous reds. Foreign, yet familiar. A beautiful stranger. He'd thrown on a battered leather jacket over his T-shirt, lending him the air of a louche model from an expensive magazine. He wore his beauty with no apology, just as he made no apology for the business he'd chosen for himself. He was a man totally at ease in his own skin, and seemed to live a life without compromise or convention. Sophie couldn't help but envy him.

He eased the car to a stop outside her house; he hadn't asked where she lived and it came as no surprise that he already knew. He'd taken one look at her and seemed to see her innermost secrets, some of which were so deep that she hadn't even been aware of them herself.

"Home sweet home," he murmured as he idled the engine. "Are you going to ask me in for coffee?"

The idea of Lucien inside her house, inside Dan's house,

horrified Sophie. To see him sit in Dan's chair… drink from Dan's cup… it was just too wrong. Inviting him over the threshold blurred all the lines, made him part of their marriage rather than in the distinct space Sophie had set aside for him in her mind.

"Or you could just ask me in for sex. I prefer sex to coffee."

"Lucien…" she sighed and twisted her fingers in her lap. "Lucien, I can't work for you anymore. This is all such a mess." She shook her head and stared out of the window, lips pursed. "I can't believe I've done any of this."

He twisted to face her, but she refused to meet his gaze.

"You're wrong," he said. "The mistake would be for you to scuttle back under your rock and hide from who you really are."

Anger licked hot inside her.

"Oh come on, Lucien. What do you *really* know about me?" This man didn't really know her, not in any way that mattered. Their relationship had followed none of the conventional routes; he knew her intimately and yet barely at all.

But then there was the sex. Oh God, the sex.

"I know enough. I know you've felt more alive in the last couple of days than you have for a long time. You were on pilot light when you came to me. Now…" he shrugged. "Now, you're blazing."

Sophie closed her eyes against the tears that threatened. She wasn't given to crying, but being around Lucien seemed to intensify all of her emotions. He definitely made her come ten times more powerfully than she'd ever known before. She groaned and pushed the heels of her palms into her eyes and rubbed hard.

She couldn't lie. He was right. Maybe she had been drifting through her married life in a state of unknowing unfulfillment, but that didn't excuse her behaviour. She cringed at the idea of herself in the club, in that room, watching those women have sex, with Lucien's erection nestled in her hand.

"Go inside, Sophie, get some sleep." He gunned the engine.

"We start after lunch again tomorrow. Don't be late."

Sophie already knew enough to realise that there was little point in arguing with him. She needed to escape into the sanctuary of her own four walls, to get Lucien and his flash car off her driveway.

He clearly didn't believe she could resist him.

He was wrong. She wasn't going back to work at Knight Inc. tomorrow, or ever again.

Lucien watched Sophie walk up her garden path, dishevelled and delicious. He couldn't help her fight the battle that raged inside her head right now; he understood that she needed to be alone tonight to work her feelings out for herself.

He turned the engine over and eased the car away without glancing back. She'd be back in his office come two o'clock tomorrow. She just didn't know it yet.

Chapter Twelve

Inside the house, Sophie locked the door and leaned her back against it, unsure her legs would hold her up much longer. She'd changed so much since she'd left home yesterday lunchtime.

The flashing red light on the answer-phone caught her eye, and she dragged in a sharp, painful breath.

It had to be Dan. She crossed and sat on the floor next to the hall table and pressed the button, her head in her hands.

"Hey Soph..." Just the sound of his voice brought a heavy pain to Sophie's chest. "It's me... where are you, babe? I really wanted to hear your voice tonight, it's been a fucking long day... I miss you... it's all pretty crap here... the usual shit. Bob's being a dick as usual with unreasonable demands and screwing up the negotiations... anyway..." he sighed audibly down the line, and Sophie squeezed her eyes tight shut.

"Wish you were here. Or I was there. Whichever... Love you, babe. See you soon, yeah?"

The message clicked off, and Sophie gulped for air as tears streamed down her face. She reached up and pressed rewind, hearing more from Dan's lengthy silences than his words. He sounded desolate.

Where had she been when he'd needed to hear her voice? She checked the recording time on the machine. *Eight o'clock.* Fresh hot tears of shame coursed down her cheeks. She couldn't bear to think of Dan standing somewhere, alone, hoping she'd pick up, when all along she'd been at The Gateway Club letting Lucien fuck her with his big silver vibrator. She wanted to scratch her own eyes out with shame as she headed straight upstairs, shedding her clothes as she went and chucking them in a ball on the landing. All except for her knickers, which were still in Lucien's pocket.

She swallowed hard, sick with disgust at herself as she stepped under the steaming shower. For well over ten minutes she stood stock-still with her face turned up into the sting of the spray, hoping it could wash away her shame along with the film of sweat that still lay on her skin from the club.

She was sleazy. She squeezed half the bottle of shower gel into her hands and scrubbed herself, gritting her teeth against the sensation of her hands on her breasts. Even touching herself brought back uncomfortable memories of Lucien's hands on her.

"No. No. No." The sound wrenched out of Sophie's chest, an animal cry of frustration as she thumped her fists against the tiled wall. She refused to let the memory dictate that it had felt good. It should have been hideous because he wasn't Dan.

Tears mingled with the shower spray on Sophie's face as she soaped her body harshly. She was shabby, and filthy, and she'd made a mockery of her wedding vows. *And for what? A fumble with a stranger in a sex club? What kind of woman did that make her?* How had Lucien so effortlessly managed to reduce her to her sexual essence, to reveal a woman inside that she didn't even recognise? A woman with kinks and perversions, a woman without sexual inhibition or respect for the sanctity of her marriage.

But then, wouldn't *any* woman have crumbled as easily, faced with the Viking force of Lucien Knight and his crusade for the sexual liberation of unfulfilled wives?

Wouldn't the threads of *anyone's* relationship have been unpicked by the nimble fingers of such a beautiful, charismatic man?

Wouldn't *every* woman have discovered her dark, carnal side when faced with Lucien? Or was she just an emotional lightweight?

Burdened by guilt, Sophie slid down the wall and let the shower rain onto her bowed head. It was hopeless. No amount of water could cleanse away the self-loathing from her skin and her self.

It didn't even matter at that moment that Dan might be screwing someone else, because the horrible truth was that it would have changed nothing. From the moment she'd kissed that envelope and posted off her job application, Sophie had set the seal on her affair with Lucien Knight.

She passed out soon after her head hit the pillow, exhausted physically by Lucien and mentally by guilt. She'd expected to toss and turn, so was surprised to find herself blinking against the spindly fingers of dull morning light as they crept between the hastily dragged-together curtains.

The alarm clock beside the bed informed her that it was a little after nine. She could get up, but her bones and her heart felt too heavy. She wanted to close her eyes and stay in bed, in her own bed, until she felt like herself again.

How long would that take? A couple of days? A few weeks? A lifetime? Sophie turned on her side and pulled the quilt over her shoulder, rolling herself into a cocoon against the outside world. She might not be able to spend forever in bed, but she could damn well spend this morning there, and this afternoon too if she felt like it, because she had no intention of going anywhere near Knight Inc.

Had Derek already filled her old job? The idea of going back, cap in hand to him, made Sophie burrow even deeper into the quilt with misery, but at least it would be a step towards pulling her life back from the brink of disaster. She closed her eyes and forced herself to breathe deeply. In. Out. In. Out. Sleep crept back through her bones, and Sophie relaxed gratefully into it. In. Out. In. Out.

And that was when the telephone rang.

Sophie sat on the bottom stair and pressed rewind on the answering machine for the third time. Dan's secretary's panic-tinged voice broke the silence again.

"Hi Dan, it's Elise… I'm so sorry to bother you when you're on holiday, Bob's having one of his emergencies." Elise's dramatic sigh spoke volumes. "Do you have any idea where the Matteson report is? Please say yes. I can't find it anywhere and he needs it for a meeting in ten minutes. You know how he gets. Call me if you can. I tried your mobile but it's off so I was just hoping you might be around at home. Sorry again."

The line clicked as Elise hung up, and Sophie slumped against the wall. *Dan wasn't on holiday. Why would he be on holiday?* He was supposed to be in Milan for negotiations. *With Bob.* But Elise would know that, wouldn't she? There could be no mistake. There was no imaginable possibility of a misunderstanding.

Sophie frowned, and rewound the messages back a few days to listen to Dan. She dropped her head in her hands as his voice washed around the empty hallway. Dan. Her Dan. *Someone else's Dan.* He talked of Bob as if he were with him, but now she knew better. She couldn't explain this away, the conclusion was obvious. He was actually on holiday with his mistress. Shock stole the air from Sophie's lungs.

She might have lost her claim to the moral high ground the moment she'd let Lucien touch her, but this thing of Dan's… it was different. If they were on holiday, if he was lying to work… it was a proper relationship. *Jesus, did he love her, whoever she was?*

Scalding tears fell down Sophie's cheeks at the idea of Dan saying those precious, sacred words to someone else.

He had always been her anchor, but too many months of burying her head in the sand over suspicions of his infidelity had cut her adrift until she'd floated too far away from him to reach out for his hand.

Drifting aimlessly, she'd reached instead for the hand of a big sexy Viking with lust coursing through his veins.

A heavy blanket of sadness settled around her shoulders. Her marriage was broken. Images of Dan and some faceless woman scrolled through her mind. A brunette in a restaurant. A blonde on a beach. A redhead in his bed.

Who was she? Who was the woman Dan had decided was worth more than their marriage vows? Sadness slid sideways into a solid wall of anger. Boiling hot rage that curdled in her gut like rancid infection.

How dare he? How fucking dare Dan trample on her love, for all these weeks and months, years even, for all Sophie knew. Her own guilt melted away under the heat of her anger. This was his fault.

This. Was. His. Fault.

Sophie's eyes flicked upwards towards the clock. Midday.

With a resolve she didn't know she possessed, she turned her mobile off and headed upstairs to change. She didn't intend on being late for work.

Chapter Thirteen

Lucien took one look at Sophie's face as she came through the door just before two o clock that afternoon and knew straight away that something had changed.

For one, she'd obviously been crying. For another, there was a new light in her eyes; something bold and determined. But by far the most telling sign of all was the stuffed-looking weekend bag she carried over her arm.

"Well, hello, Ms. Black," he flicked an eyebrow up. "I like you and all, but I'm not sure I'm ready to move in together."

She didn't laugh, just dropped the bag inside the door.

"You asked me to stay with you until Sunday. I'm all yours."

He nodded and tapped the end of the pencil on the desk as he appraised the challenging jut of her chin and her poker straight back. She was furious with someone, and the fact that she was here meant it wasn't him.

"Are you sure Mr. Tibbles can survive without you?" He flicked a lazy, speculative eyebrow upwards in question.

She sighed heavily.

"It's become abundantly clear to me that no one gives a damn where I am this week, Lucien."

Ouch. It would seem that her dickhead husband had grown lazy in his efforts to cover his tracks. Poor Princess.

"Sit down, Sophie."

She looked momentarily wrong-footed, and then sat down opposite him. Today she reminded him of a frightened young horse, skittering and wary-eyed, a world away from the woman he'd seduced at the club last night.

"Do you want to talk about it?"

She sighed again and her shoulders slumped.

"There's not much to say. Yesterday I thought my husband was having an affair. Today I know he is."

Lucien nodded. "Knowledge is power, Sophie."

"Is it?" Her anguished eyes came up to meet his. "It doesn't feel powerful. It feels like shit."

"Yet here you are."

"I'm not proud of it, Lucien. I'm not proud of the fact that I want to hurt him back."

This wasn't right. She needed to do this for herself, not her husband. Lucien spoke with feeling.

"Don't do this to hurt him, Sophie. Do it for you. Do it because you deserve better. Do it because you're beautiful." He leaned forward emphatically. "Do it because you damn well want to, and then on Sunday, you go back to him and call the fucking shots."

She hadn't taken her eyes off him as he spoke, and he'd watched the emotions play across her face.

Disbelief. Pain. Resolve. *Christ, she was exquisite.* He was going to screw her ten different ways until she couldn't stand up, and then send her home to wipe the floor with that man.

Sophie went through the motions at her desk, looking for comfort in the familiarity of switching on the computer and clearing emails and post methodically. She'd been so certain that coming into work was the best thing, and now she was here she was almost as certain that it was a huge mistake.

Lucien Knight bewitched her. Despite the riot of emotions she'd been through since he'd dropped her home last night, she'd only had to look at him this morning and lust had snaked through her veins.

Jesus, he made her feel good. He had a way of looking at her that wiped out everything else around him, whether they were alone in his office or in the middle of the packed Gateway Club.

The computer pinged, heralding the arrival of the chat message box.

"Have you taken a vow of silence, Ms. Black?"

Sophie shook her head and lifted her eyes to the ceiling.

"I'm busy."

"And I'm thirsty."

She sighed loud enough for Lucien to hear, and then crossed to the coffee machine. Lucien leaned back on his chair, and Sophie struggled to maintain her relaxed composure while she was hyper-aware of his eyes on her bottom. The cup rattled slightly in its saucer as she carried it through and deposited it on Lucien's desk.

"Is there anything in particular that you'd like me to do today, Mr. Knight?"

The lascivious gleam in his sapphire eyes told Sophie of the multitude of answers he was considering. She breathed in heavily and glanced pointedly out of the window, but she still heard the deep rumble of his laughter.

"As a matter of fact, Ms. Black, there is, yes."

Sophie dropped her gaze warily back to his and waited for him to elaborate. She couldn't second-guess him. He was just as likely to ask her for a saucy massage as for last months cash projection.

"A new supplier has sent over the demo file of their latest products. Could you review it please?"

Sophie nodded with a tight smile. She could do that. She could watch a product video and report back. "Of course." She inclined her head and backed away towards the sanctuary of her office.

"And Sophie? I want you to listen carefully to the product descriptions and pick your three favourites."

Sophie frowned. "Lucien, honestly, please don't rely on my input to choose stock. I've no clue with this stuff."

"I know that. You're not choosing stock." He shook his head, that dirty gleam still in his eyes. "You're choosing tonight's entertainment."

Sophie's mouth dropped in a perfect O, and she turned on her heel and scooted back to her desk before he could see the blush on her cheeks.

An hour later, Sophie gulped hard and clicked open the file that Lucien had forwarded. She wasn't sure what to expect, but how bad could it be? It was a corporate presentation, after all. She turned the sound down in the hope that he wouldn't realise that she was watching it, close as he sat outside her office door. The idea of him knowing she was in here looking at sex toy videos felt wrong, as if she were watching porn at her desk when she should be adding up spreadsheets. Except for the fact that she was paid to do precisely this stuff. She needed to get over her hang-ups, and fast, or she might as well give up and go home. She clicked the volume back up to normal levels and pressed play.

The screen went black, then a second or two later the sensuous silhouette of a couple having sex appeared. She glanced sharply towards the door, and then back at the screen. *She could do this*. It was pretty tame stuff, really. And it was, at least for the first few minutes. Sophie relaxed a little as she watched the managing director of the company talk about reducing their carbon footprint and the natural qualities of their products. Sophie had been expecting lurid neon plastic, so she was pleasantly surprised by the attention that the company had paid to making their toys appealing to the eye and conscience as well as the body.

The screen faded to black again, and then three words materialised. *Chris and Jeannie.*

Sophie tipped her head to the side as a different, hotter guy appeared on screen with something pale turquoise and oval shaped in his hand. What was it? Smooth and curved, it lay innocuously along the length of his palm.

A woman slipped onto the seat next to him and slid a finger along the blue petal with a smile, and then leaned in to kiss him on the mouth. She broke away after a few seconds and sat up slightly on the bench to bunch her skirt up around her waist, revealing to the camera that she wore no knickers, and also that she was completely shaved.

The guy moved to straddle behind her and dropped a tender kiss on her neck, then looked up at the camera again with a smile.

"I love to use the petal with my wife. It looks pretty innocent, doesn't it?"

Jeannie laughed and opened her legs a little wider. "It might look it, but it feels anything but innocent when Chris uses it on me."

Chris's arms slid around his wife, the petal in one hand, the other hand coming to rest on her inner thigh.

Jeannie leaned her head back against her husband's shoulder and closed her eyes, and Chris looked up at the camera again.

"To switch it on, just apply pressure to the centre of the petal."

A low buzzing hummed from the speakers of Sophie's computer as he turned it on, and Jeannie smiled with a low moan of anticipation. He turned his hand up to the screen to show the petal vibrating lightly, a gentle heart shape that stretched along his palm. Jeannie reached an arm up around her husband's neck, opening her body fully for his touch.

Chris turned his head to kiss her arm, and then touched the tip of the petal between her legs. Jeannie moaned with pleasure as Chris moved the petal down the length of her sex, his other hand fondling her breasts. Jeannie arched into his hands, and he responded, flattening the petal between her lips and covering it with his palm.

Sophie watched, mesmerised. Chris rocked the petal with two fingers, the wider paddle top vibrating on Jeannie's clitoris as the lower tip dipped inside her with every nudge of Chris's middle finger. He kissed Jeannie's ear, slowly and tenderly, then glanced up at the camera. "See how the petal fits perfectly over Jeannie? The vibrations are more intense here," he pushed his index finger against the top of the petal and held it hard against Jeannie's clitoris, making her gasp and moan. "And here." He pushed his middle finger against the lower tip instead and the camera tracked in to show a detailed shot of the petal as it slipped inside Jeannie's vagina. Chris's fingers rocked the petal expertly against his wife, making her groans heavier and her body arch.

"She's almost there," Chris murmured, and the camera panned out to show Jeannie with her eyes tight shut and her bottom lip snagged between her teeth. Chris palmed the petal and held it hard between Jeannie's legs, and she cried out as her body jerked for several moments with the intensity of her orgasm. Chris held his wife fast until she eventually opened her eyes and smiled languidly at the camera, every inch the cat that got the cream.

"The petal does it for me every time," she purred. "It's good when I'm alone, and even better with Chris."

The camera shot moved out to show the couple content in their embrace, his hand still holding the petal flat against her sex.

"Open your drawer."

The message from Lucien popped up in the instant chat box in the corner of the screen, making Sophie start with guilt. She looked at her closed drawer. Then opened it. Pale blue and pretty, the petal sat nestled in its tissue wrapping.

"A gift for you."

Sophie swallowed and picked up the petal. It felt even better than she'd imagined. Substantial, but tactile.

"Do you like it?"

Sophie found she couldn't breathe as easily as usual.

"Yes."

"I'm imagining you using it on yourself right now."

Dear God. Sophie swallowed, because she'd been imagining the same thing.

"Yes."

"Naughty Sophie. You're at work."

Sophie nodded, more to herself than him.

"If I came in there right now and slipped my hand up your skirt, I think you'd be wet and ready for me."

Sophie froze with her fingers above the keyboard. She couldn't think of a single word to type in response. She heard his low, dirty laugh and had to fight the urge to go through there right now and straddle him at his desk.

He continued the exchange without waiting for her to respond.

"Hold that thought for later and watch the rest of the video."

She wanted to lay her head on the desk and cry with frustration.

"Yes, Mr. Knight."

"And Sophie? Remember. Three things. Make a list. I'm going to make you come harder than Jeannie and more times than you can count.

Chapter Fourteen

A little after five, Sophie heard Lucien's office door open. He'd been downstairs in a meeting for most of the afternoon, leaving her free to tussle with her conscience and watch the video as instructed and construct her list of three items.

She'd squirmed her way through most of it, shocked at times, horrified occasionally, but more than anything else she was turned on and desperate for Lucien.

She smiled tensely as he appeared around her doorway.

"Good meeting?"

He shrugged. "I got what I wanted, so yes."

Sophie drew in a deep breath. It seemed that this man always got what he wanted, in business and in pleasure.

"Have you made your list?"

Sophie automatically glanced down at the scrap of paper on her desk. She had indeed made the list he'd requested, but not without considerable discomfort. Just writing the words had made her blush. Lucien's gaze followed hers, and he crossed the room and picked the piece of paper up. He scanned it in silence for what felt to Sophie like at least three hours.

"Interesting choices, Ms. Black. A little tame in places, but we can work on that." He unfastened the top button on his shirt and ran a finger around the collar. For one shocking - no, thrilling - second Sophie thought he was going to start working on it right there and then, but he turned away and headed for the door.

"Finish up, Sophie. We're leaving."

Sophie glanced at Lucien's profile as he drove. He handled the car with the same mastery with which he managed everything else in his life, and it responded to his touch like a rapt lover. She had no clue where they were headed, but she was relieved from the direction he'd taken that it wasn't the club again.

She could ask him, of course, but it didn't matter really, because she'd made the decision to give herself over to him completely until Sunday. There was a certain freedom in following his lead; freedom from responsibility, the surrender of all conscious decision.

They were out in open countryside now, which surprised her. Lucien was such a creature of the metropolis, he belonged in the dark, throbbing glass and metal heart of the city. He looked out of place here amongst rolling fields and lush hedgerows.

He turned sharply along an unmarked road and a pair of black iron gates swung silently open to allow them access.

It was a stark contrast to last night when he'd dropped her home in her suburban cul-de-sac. He steered along the sweeping driveway, and as the car rounded the bend, Sophie caught her first glimpse of what had to be his home. The location had lulled her into expecting a country house, so the breathtaking front wall of Lucien's thoroughly modern country pad was a revelation. An architect's wet dream of juxtaposed angles and sheet glass, it was more of a sculpture than a home.

"Wow."

He turned to look at her as the engine idled whilst he waited for the garage door to slide silently upwards.

"Not what you were expecting?"

"No… actually, it's just what I was expecting, but in an unexpected place."

He slid the car inside the garage and climbed out.

"Out here, no one can hear you scream, Ms. Black."

Sophie got out of the passenger side and eyed him across the roof of the Aston Martin. She wasn't frightened. For some reason she knew she could trust him. She would never have come here if she wasn't utterly sure that she would be safe. He would protect her, not harm her.

He was right about one thing, though. There was every chance he was going to make her scream.

Chapter Fifteen

Sophie followed Lucien into the house and found herself in a huge, sunken lounge, which, from the angles of the windows, appeared to be cut into the hillside. Lush, warm wood tones complemented the oversized mink velvet couches. Classy and understated with huge rugs and sleek furniture, it screamed sexy urbanity, with its theatrical mood lighting and floor to ceiling glass. All very in keeping with the man who stood beside her.

"Make yourself at home. I'll be back in a few seconds."

He stroked a hand down the zip that ran the length of her spine as he spoke, making her shiver with anticipation. She'd chosen today's outfit with care, knowing that she was going to him with the intention of staying.

Kara's royal blue dress fitted her snugly around the bodice, its three quarter sleeves a demure contrast with its scooped neckline. The skirt flared around her thighs and ended just above her knees, and she'd opted for high heels, bare legs and her favourite French navy lace underwear. It felt flirtatious, a deliberate decision to signify her intent to Lucien, and a reminder to herself - if she needed one - not to back out.

Left momentarily to her own devices, she glanced around the room for traces of the real Lucien. There was nothing. No photographs, no knick-knacks, no tell-tale little giveaways. It could have been anyone's home, apart from the fact that it somehow sung out his name from its very bricks and mortar.

He sauntered back into the room, having changed from his dark work clothes into battered jeans and nothing else. Sophie closed her eyes and sucked in her breath. He really was beautiful, all broad golden shoulders and hard, lean muscle. He was barefoot, and Sophie knew without needing to check that there would be no underwear beneath those jeans.

Lucien placed three items on the coffee table with deliberate care, glancing up at her between each one to gauge her reaction. As soon as the first item appeared, Sophie's pulse skittered, because she knew exactly what to expect next.

A black silk blindfold.

A glass dildo, more shimmering art than sex toy.

And last of all, a heavy silver acorn-shaped butt plug on a rocking stand.

"Your list, I believe, Ms. Black."

Sophie looked at the items. *Had she really chosen a butt plug?* Jeannie had seemed to love it, and Sophie had been too lathered up thinking about Lucien to consider fully the reality of him working it into her own backside.

Lucien crossed the room to stand behind her, and seconds later Sophie felt his fingers slide her zip down in one fluid movement.

"You need to relax, Sophie."

He let the dress slip to the floor, leaving her standing in only her underwear and high heels. How could she possibly relax in this state? He'd deliberately pushed her buttons all afternoon, no doubt knowing that she would be putty in his hands by the time he got her here. He turned her in his arms, and she found her stomach against the warm, hard silk of his.

His hands slid into her hair as he drew her face up to his, tilting her mouth to take his kiss. His lips went from gentle to insistent to a full on sensual assault in seconds, leaving her reeling when he lifted his head. His eyes burned into hers and his hands stole up to pull her bra cups down. He pinched her nipples into hard nubs.

"See? Isn't that better?"

Frankly, Sophie wasn't sure she felt any more relaxed, but she didn't want him to stop, so she pushed her arms together and reached down to massage Lucien's crotch. She looked down at her cleavage, her exposed pink nipples erect and begging for his attention. Lucien eyes closed momentarily as her hands circled his erection, then snapped open and locked with hers. He rocked his denim-clad cock forward into her hands.

"I'm going to fuck you until you can't stand up," he said softly.

Excitement pooled between Sophie's legs as she popped the top button of his jeans. Lucien shook his head and stepped away. "But not yet."

He picked up the blindfold from the table.

"I'm guessing this was the first thing you picked."

Sophie nodded and swallowed hard.

"Because you thought it was the safest choice." It was a statement rather than a question.

She lifted one shoulder, unable to argue, because he was right. It had felt like the tamest choice compared to most of the items she'd seen that afternoon.

"You didn't think this through at all, Princess," he murmured as he stepped in front of her again. "Blindfolds are all about control. Or loss of it." He placed the black silk over her eyes and tied it lightly behind her head. Sophie closed her eyes behind the material, disoriented by the darkness. She could hear Lucien moving, but couldn't get a fix on where he was without her vision to help her.

"Lucien, please. I don't think I'm ready yet…" she murmured, anxiety spiking through her body. She wanted to reach up and adjust her bra. And then she didn't want to, because his hot mouth fastened around one nipple and sucked, and his fingers rolled the other hard tip. The shock of not realising he'd been so close made her cry out, and a bolt of lust slashed suddenly through her insides.

She reached out for him, but he caught her arms and put them back at her sides. "When you're blindfolded, you don't touch me unless I say so."

What? Dan had never been a dominant lover, and Lucien's

authority thrilled her far more than she liked to admit.

"This is how it has to be when you're blindfolded, Sophie." He whispered, behind her now, and he pushed his hand unexpectedly down the front of her knickers.

"Fuck, Lucien!" Sophie gasped, beyond turned on by his erotic game.

"That's not very polite, is it, Ms. Black?" His fingers delved deeper until his hand cupped her sex. "The second rule of being blindfolded," he whispered as he parted her and pushed two fingers inside her, "is that you must be polite at all times."

Sophie nodded. "Yes, Mr. Knight." Christ, his fingers felt amazing. She couldn't help but rock herself against him, and she yelped in shock when his other hand smacked her bottom really quite hard.

"Did I give you permission to enjoy it?"

Sophie couldn't get her breath. When he'd smacked her it had forced his fingers deeper inside her, and all she could think was *do it again, do it again, do it again.* "No, Mr. Knight."

"That's better." His hand fondled her bottom to soothe away the sting, then he eased his other hand out of her knickers. "I'm going to take the blindfold off for now. When I put it on again later, I want you to remember the rules. Can you do that, Sophie?"

Sophie nodded.

His palm slapped her bottom again. "Out loud, if you please, Ms. Black."

Sophie deliberated for a second as he massaged her again. *Did she please?* If she didn't say it out loud, it was becoming apparent that there would be consequences. It appeared that hesitation was another forbidden sin, because Lucien tutted under his breath with clear impatience. Sophie braced herself.

"You have much to learn, Princess." His voice was silk against her ear as his palm stung the cheek of her bottom for a third time. Zings of pain and pleasure fired between Sophie's legs. It felt wrong to want him to do it again, but every nerve in her body screamed out for more.

She almost grumbled out loud in frustration when his fingers slipped the knot on the blindfold open. Sophie blinked as her eyes readjusted to the light, and her body mourned the loss of his touch.

When she turned around, she saw Lucien standing with his arms folded across his bare chest and the gleam of triumph in his eyes.

"It would seem that blindfolds aren't quite as innocent as you thought, Sophie."

"I don't think there were any innocent choices on that video, Lucien."

"Maybe not. Take your bra off."

"Lucien…" Embarrassed, Sophie looked down at her half exposed breasts, wanting to pull the material back into place rather than take it off. He reached out and pulled her against him, shockingly warm, skin to skin, his evident erection hard against her stomach.

He looked down at her. "You feel what you do to me?"

He traced a slow finger from one puckered nipple to the other, then reached behind her and unclipped her bra. The material fell away, leaving Sophie almost naked and vulnerable in his arms. He dipped his head to claim her mouth, his lips warm and gentle on hers. Slow. Sensual.

His arms moved to hold her against him, her breasts crushed against the wall of his chest. Sophie clung to him, wiped out by the tenderness of his kiss. "Princess," he whispered against her lips, his hands between their bodies to cradle the fullness of her breasts.

"Lucien…" she breathed, swept away by how good his hands made her feel. He reached down and lifted her clean off her feet, and she wrapped her legs around his waist as his hands cupped her bottom. She revelled in the sensation of his strength around her softness. They both groaned in response to the way her sex cradled his erection, and he moved her slightly to accommodate him fully between her legs. His mouth never left hers as he crossed the room to lay her down on the plump cushions of the sofa. He covered her body with his own, and Sophie sighed with primal satisfaction at his weight over hers.

From the moment she'd met Lucien he'd radiated danger and lust, but right at that moment, cocooned beneath the warmth of his chest, he gave her the last thing she expected, and it turned out to be the thing she needed most of all. He gave her safe harbour. She felt protected in his arms.

She hadn't anticipated how incredibly sweet his kiss could be, or how gentle his hands might be as they slid her knickers down her legs. There was no talk of blindfolds, no glance towards the toys lined up on the table. Sophie sensed that this was probably outside of Lucien's plan, and she treasured him all the more for understanding what she needed. The breath jarred in her throat as his fingers moved to unbutton his jeans. For all that had happened between them, she'd yet to see him naked. The final barrier. He reached into his pocket for a condom, and then kicked his jeans off.

For a few seconds, Lucien simply settled his body over the length of hers and held her, giving her time to accept the weight of his erection against her abdomen. Sophie melted. *She wanted him. Christ she wanted him.* There was no doubt, there were no second thoughts. Lucien had kissed them all away. He ripped the foil packet of the condom with his teeth and sheathed himself, then settled back between her legs with his forearms either side of her head.

"Open your eyes," he murmured as his knee moved between hers. Sophie lifted her lashes, and Lucien's clear blue gaze locked with hers as he tipped his hips slowly, his rock hard length stoking delicious friction back and forth over her clitoris. "Feel good?" A lazy half smile touched his lips. Sophie bit down on her lip to hold the cry of pleasure inside. This man was something else when it came to confidence. *Jesus, yes. You know it feels good.*

Lucien's tender thumbs stroked the rogue tears from her

cheeks, and his feather kisses traced her lips as he positioned himself.

Sophie clutched him, her fingernails digging arcs into his shoulders. He was strength, and he was magnificence, and as his beautiful hard cock sliced decisively into her, he became her Viking lover. Sophie cried out his name as he filled her, foreign and mysterious, and each thrust sent lust spiralling higher, tighter, deeper… more, more, more. Euphoria mingled with physical pleasure, building with Lucien's every stroke and thrust.

More. More. More. Boneless and mindless, she was a pool of heat and desire underneath his mastery.

His hand cupped her face as his other snaked between their damp bodies, and Sophie gulped in dry air as he thumbed her clitoris. Thrust. Stroke. Rub. Thrust. Stroke. Rub. He set up a trinity of motion, and with every repetition he pushed Sophie closer and closer towards the edge of control.

His eyes still held her gaze, and she could see the effort in his clenched jaw as he held his own pleasure back for hers. His thumb was still stroking her clitoris, and his tongue mirrored the movement in her mouth.

"You. Are. Fucking. Amazing," he ground out, punctuating each word with a deeper thrust. Sophie's fingers curved around his nape as her hips started to buck uncontrollably, and Lucien read her cues well and switched from slow and deep to fast and hard. His tongue in her mouth, his cock buried inside her. *Faster, harder, yes, yes, yes!* Sophie's orgasm exploded through her body, making her shudder and jolt beneath him. Lucien threw his head back and pumped his hips, leaving her nowhere to go but further over the top with him. They moved in frenzied, primal unison.

Animal.

Feral.

Sensational.

Lucien rested his forehead against Sophie's, the aftermath of his orgasm still vibrating through his groin. He hadn't intended this to happen in quite such a vanilla way, but one look at at Sophie's vulnerable face and his hunter-protector gene had kicked in hard. Most of all he'd wanted to settle her, to comfort her, to gentle rather than shock her into submission.

He kissed the tip of her nose. Shocking her was next on his agenda.

Chapter Sixteen

Sophie wound the belt of the short, white towelling robe around her waist and knotted it, glad that Lucien had been thoughtful enough to provide it. He had slid back into his battered jeans. The toys still sat central on the coffee table, and she did her best not to look in their direction as she padded through to the open plan kitchen after Lucien.

Pristine white gloss and stainless steel units lined the walls in unbroken ranks; it was clear to Sophie that this wasn't a kitchen that saw much in the way of action. Or not cooking, at least.

It was a little after nine, and dusk had turned the sky outside a deep petrol blue and the trees around the house into spindled black shadows. Not quite night time, but almost there. Sophie sensed, with a minute thrill, that it would nonetheless be a long time until bedtime.

As she entered the kitchen, Lucien was standing with his back towards her, lit by the soft light from inside the huge stainless steel fridge he was reaching into. She was pulled up sharply by the beautiful monochrome tattoo inked across his broad shoulders.

An intricately detailed lone wolf, bound around with ropes and vines stretched from shoulder blade to shoulder blade, enhancing every slope and taut angle of his back. It was stunning, and Sophie longed to go and run her hands over it. Over him. He turned as she approached, and she lost her nerve.

"Hungry?"

Sophie thought about it and decided that in actual fact, she was starving.

"Yes. Yes, I am. Is this where you tell me you're a crack hot chef?"

Lucien lifted a lazy eyebrow.

"No. This is the point where I offer to serve you sushi off my navel."

Sophie's eyes opened wide. *Was he even joking?* She still didn't have a good enough measure of him to be sure. She breathed a sigh of relief when he retrieved a huge bacon quiche, a bag of salad and a bottle of champagne from the fridge and closed the door.

"We're in luck. Fran has been today."

Fran? Who was Fran?

Lucien heaped food onto two plates without offering an explanation. To be fair, he didn't owe her one. He was her boss, and her one week only lover, nothing more.

The food was delicious, helped down by champagne that loosened both Sophie's nerves and her tongue. Was Fran his girlfriend? His lover? His mother? She burned to know. *Jesus, was she his wife?*

No. He wasn't married. She couldn't put her finger on it, but he was most definitely single. *Unlike her.* Thoughts of Dan on holiday somewhere with his lover encroached on her mind, and she began to push her food listlessly around the plate.

"Stop it," Lucien said softly.

Her eyes flickered up.

"Ditch the guilt, Sophie."

Boy, he was good. He might be unreadable to her, but to him, she seemed to be an open book.

"It's not that easy." She picked up her champagne glass and drank deeply, trying to wash away the melancholy.

Lucien filled up her glass again.

"Your husband doesn't seem to struggle with it."

The melancholy twisted into anger. Lucien was right. Dan hadn't given her a second thought when he'd planned his clandestine holiday. *Christ… what if he wasn't coming back? Had he left her and just couldn't find the balls to tell her?*

She shut her eyes. What a mess. Why was she here? What did it prove, really? That anything Dan could do, she could do better? Because one thing was for sure. Whatever Dan had done, she was going to do far worse before Sunday rolled around.

"So, Sophie. I'm intrigued." Lucien said conversationally, breaking her train of thought. "Why the glass dildo?"

Lucien directed Sophie upstairs to his bedroom whilst he grabbed a fresh bucket of ice and a bottle of vodka from the freezer. He pocketed the blindfold and the metal acorn as he passed through the lounge, plunging the glass dildo into the ice bucket as he headed for the stairs.

In a late night bar in Greece, Dan ordered another brandy just to annoy Maria. She objected to him drinking too much in case he couldn't perform in bed. Nothing like Sophie, who happily matched him drink for drink then loved to slide tipsily into a late night game of strip poker. Or else she used to, back when they were happy. *Where had it all gone so wrong?*

He looked up as Maria wound her way back across the bar. Brunette instead of blonde. Gym-firm instead of softly curved.

She smiled when she caught his eye, and then pinched her brows together when he saluted her with his refreshed brandy glass. *Whatever.*

Sophie lingered in the doorway of Lucien's vast bedroom. More floor to ceiling glass, but by now the view was hidden beneath the velvet cloak of the black night sky. A huge, metal-framed bed dominated the central space of the room, covered in snowy white sheets, plump cushions, and throws fashioned from neutral velvets and furs. Den-like. The hairs on the back of Sophie's neck prickled at the thought of spending the night in it with Lucien.

The rest of the room was almost clinically tidy, the sleek

wooden walls and floors disrupted only by a huge sheepskin rug. This was very much Lucien's lair, and Sophie felt for a moment as a lamb to the slaughter. She moved across and perched on the edge of the bed at the sound of Lucien coming upstairs, and noted with apprehension that there were mirrors on the ceiling over his bed. It seemed curiously old hat, a kind of borderline lazy way for a love god to mark out his territory.

"Refreshments," he said, placing the ice bucket down. "And entertainment." He dropped the blindfold onto the bedside table and laid the silver acorn next to it. He flicked a lighter to a candle, then turned to face her. His eyes skimmed down the terry gown still wrapped tightly around her body.

"You're overdressed."

Naked beneath the robe, Sophie's pulse accelerated.

He watched her in silence for a long few seconds, and when she didn't move to undress, he reached down and flicked the top button of his own jeans open instead. Sophie blinked hard, her eyes following his fingers as he worked the second button open. She cleared her throat as he went for the third. His golden, sculpted navel gleamed in the candle glow. As he released the last button, he pushed his jeans down and stepped free of them, then straightened, buck naked and utterly nonchalant.

"See? No clothes. Easy." He spread his hands wide, and Sophie gorged on the visual feast he was offering her.

He was easily the most beautiful man she'd ever seen, in real life, or in magazines or movies. All gleaming hard planes and athletic, lean muscle. Sophie's eyes strayed lower, beyond his navel.

Christ. His cock. She pulled in her breath hard as she stared at the thick, long curve standing rigid against his abdomen. Despite the fact that she'd experienced him so intimately inside her, this was the first chance she'd had to see him fully naked. He took her breath away.

When she eventually dragged her eyes back up to his face, she found that cocky half smile back in place on his lips. He knew the effect he was having on her. He turned away.

God, how her fingers itched to touch those broad, inked shoulders, to trail down the length of his granite spine to his perfectly curved backside. Sophie puffed her fringe out of her eyes. If Lucien had been around in the Renaissance period, sculptors would have gouged out their own eyeballs for a chance to sculpt him.

He turned back around and tipped his head to one side.

"Your turn."

Sophie caught her bottom lip between her teeth, trapped between nerves and the desire to comply. Desire won. She got slowly to her feet, and Lucien moved around her to take her place on the edge of the bed. He planted his hands on the fur throw behind him, his cock looming large and shameless in front of him.

Sophie licked her dry lips and reached for the belt of the gown.

"Turn around."

She hadn't expected instruction, but accepted his request with a tingle of lust in her groin. Her back turned, she released the belt.

"Go slow."

His low command made her revise her plan to drop the robe, and she shimmied it just one shoulder off instead.

"Good girl."

Encouraged, she slid the other shoulder down, but kept hold of the robe as it slipped down her spine, holding it as a seductive cover over her bottom. She turned to throw a saucy glance at Lucien over one shoulder and found him slowly stroking the length of his hard cock with one hand.

Her jaw dropped and she turned away quickly, letting the robe fall to the floor. The knowledge that he was behind her, lazily masturbating, turned her knees to jelly, and a snake pit of nerves writhed in her gut as she willed herself to be brave. She turned back around to face him.

He didn't take his hand away from his erection as he nodded

slowly, his eyes sliding from her face to her breasts. Sophie felt her nipples pucker into ripe beads under his scrutiny, and she could barely get her breath as his eyes travelled lower. Her hands were awkward at her sides, and she knew her cheeks were pink with discomfort and desire in equal measure.

Lucien stared at her crotch and stroked himself for a second longer, then licked his lips and stood up.

His height above hers struck Sophie anew, further enhanced by the vulnerability of being naked.

"You see?" He gestured to their bodies with his hands.

"Man." He touched his fingers to his chest and raised his eyebrows.

"Woman." He brushed his fingertips over the base of her throat.

"Sex is natural." He trailed one finger down the valley between her breasts to her navel, making her stomach muscles jitter in response. "And fucking beautiful."

His clear blue eyes held hers. "Now, forget everything else," he said, "And Get. On. That. Bed." He punctuated his words with heavy pauses, turning his invitation into a desire-laden demand that Sophie was powerless to resist.

Chapter Seventeen

The fur throw was warm against Sophie's naked back as she reclined, and the softness of the mattress beckoned her in. *What a blissful bed.* Even in her heightened state of sexual anticipation, Sophie couldn't help but notice its cocoon-like warmth and comfort, in direct contrast to the dangerous man stretched out on his side next to her, holding a blindfold in his hand.

His body was close enough to touch along the length of hers from shoulder to knee, his erection heavy on her hip. If he chose to move he could be inside her within a second, and the thought set a pulse throbbing between her legs.

He trailed the silk blindfold over her skin. Across her breasts, over her stomach, hipbone to hipbone. Sophie sighed, relaxed by the whisper tease of the silk's caress.

"You remember what we said about this blindfold, Sophie?"

Lucien stroked the black silk lightly between her legs, and she opened her thighs a little. The feel of his hand hovering but not quite touching her made her breath catch in her throat.

Sophie closed her eyes for a moment, and then nodded and lifted her head. Lucien reacted immediately, placing the blindfold across her eyes and knotting it carefully in place.

When she opened her eyes and saw only darkness, for a moment panic threatened to engulf her. "Lucien?" She spoke his name out loud, and his finger touched against her lips to calm her.

"Sshh." His lips brushed hers. "Your eyes will adjust to the darkness."

Sophie drew in a shuddering breath and found he was right.

"Do I need a safe word?" she breathed anxiously, drawing something suspiciously like a laugh from Lucien.

"No, really, you don't. If you want me to stop, just say stop. But for the record… you won't."

He was too confident. His finger stayed at her lips, tracing them gently, and she opened her mouth and nipped him. He took her jaw between his fingers and held it hard.

"Don't bite me," he murmured warningly, and his hand strayed lower to encircle her throat. Sophie sucked in a breath then exhaled as she felt him lean across her body towards the bedside table. *Lord, he was warm and heavy.* She could hear a drawer scraping open. *Was he reaching for a condom already?* And then he was back beside her again and placing something unexpected in her hands.

Sophie frowned behind the blindfold as her tentative fingers learned the outline of the two slender, smooth leather circles he'd given her. They were linked by a short, cool metal chain. *Cuffs.*

"Lucien… I'm not sure about…" she whispered, but even to her own ears, her protests sounded hollow. The weight of the cuffs in her hands brought back memories of how he'd clamped her arms behind her back in the club, and she couldn't deny the fact that she'd got off on the sensation. Her fingers traced the body-warm leather, discovering the cool metal stud on each bracelet that she guessed must adjust their size to fit.

"Put your arms above your head," Lucien ordered softly.

Sophie trembled inside, but willingly offered up her hands.

The first leather circle slipped over one of her wrists and Lucien's careful fingers adjusted it so she couldn't wriggle her hand free. Anxiety prickled through Sophie's mind as she heard the chain rattle against metal, then Lucien's fingers enclosed her other wrist. She pulled back a little, feeling the effect of the restraint.

"Trust me." He murmured, and brushed his mouth over hers before returning his attention to securing the second cuff.

"There." He finished his work. "Now test them. Make sure

your hands don't slide out."

His words came out as a dark, delicious order, and Sophie wriggled her wrists. Not only could she not get the cuffs off, but Lucien had passed the chain behind the metal fretwork of the bed, locking her arms in place. Captured, she gasped and arched her back, feeling the combined thrill and shock of constraint.

Lucien's low laugh rumbled in her ear. "I'll take that as a yes, shall I? Try to relax."

Sophie wished she could. She knew her breasts must be jutting crudely upwards, but the restraints turned her on so much that she couldn't soften her spine.

She really wished she could see him. The double whammy of the loss of free movement and vision left her defenseless, and her body thrummed with erotic anticipation. Lucien was unpredictable at the best of times. With the deprivation of two of her senses, she upgraded him to downright lethal.

Endless silent seconds stretched out without him touching her, and Sophie spun round a wheel of emotions... lust... fear... anxiety... back to delicious lust again. Her body screamed for his touch, and with every moment he made her wait, her nerves tightened to snapping point.

And then came her reward. His warm, wet mouth fastened over one rock hard nipple as he traced an ice-cube around the other. She gasped out loud and arched forward even further, greedy for more. He sucked harder on her nipple until she felt it elongate in his mouth, while his fingers circled her other nipple with the ice cube. His mouth was hot. His fingers were icy. She squirmed, but the leather cuffs held her wrists firmly in place. Sophie jangled the chain against the metal bed like an unwilling prisoner, getting a sensual thrill from the rattle and the feeling of entrapment. She felt chained, totally at his mercy, and the submissive in her revelled in it. She wanted this man to do whatever he saw fit, to touch her everywhere, to possess her body in any way he wanted to.

An ice cube slid into her navel, making her suck in air sharply.

"Be still," he said, the first time he'd spoken since he'd cuffed her. "Let it melt." His hands were on her breasts, warming where she was chilled, cupping her fullness, massaging her as his tongue slid into her mouth.

The ice cube started to melt against the heat of her skin and tiny rivulets of freezing water trickled around her waist. She tried to flex her body against the ticklish drips, but Lucien moved his knee to cover her legs and hold her down.

"Be. Still."

Sophie found that she wanted to know what would happen if she disobeyed him.

She breathed out hard, forcing her stomach muscles upwards in an effort to dislodge the melting cube.

"Sophie…" he warned, low and sultry.

A salacious thrill unfurled in her belly. He'd warned her twice.

She had no clue how to play this game. Should she obey, or should she stray from compliance? What were the rules here? Dan had never lashed her to the bed and ordered her not to move while he melted ice in her belly button: this was all uncharted territory for her. The impulse to be naughty won out. She pursed her lips and flicked her hips. The ice cube flipped off her body, and she waited with bated breath.

Lucien sighed, heavily and audibly, so she couldn't miss it despite her blindfold. "Sophie. Do you *want* me to punish you?"

She bit her lip, genuinely unsure.

"I wasn't planning on it, but you're making my fingers itch to reach for the paddle in the drawer next to you."

Paddle? Okay… so maybe she should have obeyed him after all.

"No paddle," she breathed, and held her body stock still as his mouth drifted from the base of her throat to her pubic bone and back up again, his hand heavy on her thigh.

"Better," he murmured, and licked each of her nipples in turn. Long, slow sweeps of his tongue that made her moan with pleasure.

"Better still." He cupped her breasts in his hands and pushed them together with a guttural sound of appreciation.

The effort of holding still was worth it to feel and hear his approval. He had a way of taking charge of her and managing to make her feel invincible at the same time, and it was a heady combination.

When he moved away from her her anxiety levels spiked again. She jumped as his hands grasped her ankles and swept them apart, then he moved to kneel between her calves.

"If you could only see what I can see right now," he murmured.

Sophie closed her eyes behind the blindfold. He must have an x-rated view, she could feel her sex opening for him. She must be all heaving breasts and pink flesh. Am image of the lesbians from the sex club crept back into her mind and Sophie was glad of the blindfold to hide her abashed eyes from Lucien.

His palms swept up her legs, long slow strokes that ended tantalisingly close to her sex. He paused and reached across her body to the table again.

"I'm going to pour warm wax on you."

Sophie yanked hard on her restraints in shock. She'd seen Madonna do something similar in a kinky movie and it had looked painful. Lucien splayed his hand on her stomach to still her, and the remaining melted ice water in her navel spilled over her body.

"Didn't I tell you to trust me?"

Before she could find her voice to protest, Lucien had trailed a ribbon of warm droplets across her abdomen from hip to hip.

She released the breath she'd been holding in. The wax was hot but not scaldingly so, and Lucien's hands had settled over her pubic bone, a huge warm butterfly pressing gently on her flesh.

"It melts into oil," he said as his hands started to glide over her skin, his thumbs occasionally brushing the tiny landing strip of hair spared by her beauty therapist. His fingers warm and slick on her inner thighs, Lucien massaged the oil everywhere apart from where she really craved it. She splayed her legs wide and lifted her hips into his hands.

Could he see her clitoris? He must be able to. She was as open as she possibly could be to him, throbbing with lust for his hands to zero in on her sex.

Instead, he licked her.

The feel of his head nestled between her legs had her gasping his name, and in response his hands settled on her hips to hold her steady.

Sophie's head thrashed from side to side, her eyes squeezed shut beneath the silk of the blindfold. The chain on the cuffs scraped against the bed as she writhed, restless for release.

Jesus. The man knew what he was doing. His tongue was everywhere. Slow and easy over her clitoris. Long and firm as it dipped inside her. She was hot, and wet, and wanting. He was strong, and giving, and so mind-numbingly sexy that Sophie started to tremble from her tied up hands to her toes. She was going to come. *She was going to come.*

And that was when Lucien stopped.

"No!" she cried out and bucked her body towards where he had been, desperate for him to come back. And then he did, making her jump violently as something cold and hard whispered over her nipples. She felt them stiffen instantly under its icy ministrations.

What was that? It was too solid for ice. She was hot, and whatever it was, it was beyond cold. Her brain reeled with lust as he stroked the object across her mouth.

It was cold. And hard. *And glass.*

And then she knew, even as her lips parted to allow the bulbous end of the glass dildo into her mouth.

She heard Lucien groan, and could only imagine how sluttish she must look tied to the bed and letting him fuck her mouth with the big glass cock.

It was so, so cold.

Lucien slipped his other hand between her parted legs and pushed his fingers inside her, then eased the dildo out of her mouth and touched it against her clitoris instead.

Ice-cold and mouth-warm all at the same time, and hard. So very, very hard. Sophie moaned in appreciation of the brand new sensations Lucien had exposed her body to. Cold, heavy glass against fever-hot flesh.

He leaned forward and slipped his tongue into her mouth, then reached behind her head and untied the blindfold.

"Open your eyes, Princess."

Sophie blinked as her restored vision adjusted to the light, and she saw her own image reflected in the ceiling mirrors. Naked. Splayed. Chained. A Viking knelt between her knees.

The glass dildo looked even more erotic in his hands than it had on the film. Clear crystal, with a raised ribbon of glittering Aurora Borealis glass helter-skeltered around the outside… delicious ridges of friction every time he turned it, and a bulbous, cock-like end. Lucien screwed it slowly into her, and the nuances of the rippled glass bounced a million tiny rainbows of colour around the walls of the candlelit room. Still cold, Sophie felt every delicious ridge of the dildo slide in, unyielding and rock solid.

Her eyes devoured the erotic tableau. Lucien, naked and kneeling, the beautiful wolf tattoo alive across his muscular back as he worked between her legs. Soft fur at her back. Crystal rainbows on the walls. Leather cuffs around her wrists.

Sophie revised her opinion on mirrored ceilings. They weren't old hat. They were a classic for a reason.

When Lucien dipped his head to suckle her clitoris, the early warning signs of Sophie's oncoming orgasm started to tingle through her body like electricity.

Lucien, Lucien, Lucien…

Lucien glanced up Sophie's taut curves and caught her eye a second before his tongue touched her clitoris again. He'd had countless women over the years, but Sophie Black, naked and shackled to his bed, was up there with the most erotic encounters of his life. Watching her bloom made his cock ache.

She was so ready, he could feel her clitoris quivering and swollen.

It was time.

He screwed the glass dildo as deep as it would go inside her and traced letters on her clitoris with the tip of his tongue.

P…she shuddered

R…she arched

I…she moaned

N…she gasped his name

C…"Lucien..."

E…she came

S…and came

S…and she came.

Chapter Eighteen

According to the luminous clock on Lucien's bedside table, it was a little after four a.m. Sophie blinked as her eyes adjusted to the shadowed room, half awake and very aware of the weight of Lucien's arm across her body.

She turned her head on the pillow to look at him, and her fingers ached to reach out and stroke the proud slant of his cheekbone.

Sleep had robbed him of his trademark cocky smile and easy confidence, leaving him stripped bare and vulnerable as a child. There was a sweetness to the sweep of his lashes on his cheek, and an innocence to the cupid bow of his top lip. Studying him, Sophie could almost see the carefree, tearaway child he must have been. *Who was he?* How had he gone from child to man, from innocent boy to self-styled leader of a movement for sexual liberation?

His home offered no clues to his past, and the internet had proved equally unforthcoming when it came to revealing the boy behind the man.

He sighed in his sleep, and Sophie turned her body fully into the circle of his arms. He gathered her closer, and she breathed him in. Whoever he was, right now she was just glad to have him in her life.

She slept.

Lucien clicked off his mobile. All of the arrangements were in place, the work of minutes. It was one of the things he appreciated most about his wealth - it waved a magic wand and made anything possible.

He needed his private jet readied for take-off with three hours' notice? No problem.

He wanted the lodge prepared by lunchtime? Consider it done.

Money talked, for sure. But right now the only conversation he was interested in using it to facilitate was the one where Sophie realised that she held all of the aces, not her husband.

As far as he could see, marriage was all about power. His own father had held all of the cards in his parents' marriage, his mother perpetually playing a losing hand.

When Sophie had walked into his office last Monday evening, the defensive look in her eyes at the mention of her marriage had stirred deep-seated memories, decades-old echoes of a similarly haunted look in his mother's eyes.

But then, last night, that look had been nowhere to be seen on Sophie's face, especially not in the seconds before she'd come. *By the end of the weekend the look would be banished forever.*

A grim smile touched the corners of his mouth at the thought of Daniel Black returning home on Sunday. The man was in for one hell of a shock.

Sophie dashed around her suburban semi, throwing clothes and her passport into the overnight bag that lay flung open on the bed. Her home felt like a doll's house after Lucien's mansion, and just a couple of days of standing empty had lent it a forlorn air that she was anxious to escape from. Lucien had given her exactly ten minutes, and then he was turning off the engine and coming in to get her. This she did not want. He had no place here, in her home.

She had no idea where they were headed or what to pack, but instinct had her throwing in her prettiest underwear and her favourite dress and heels. Lucien had suggested she also bring a coat, so she zipped her bag and laid her cherry red wool coat on top of it. She was ready.

In her haste to get into the car before Lucien got out of it, she never noticed the flashing light on the answering machine in the hallway.

Sophie had only ever flown in economy class, so climbing aboard a private jet an hour or so later was something of a culture shock. There had been no duty free shopping or check-in queues, just a uniformed driver to take Lucien's Aston away for him as they moved straight from the car to the steps of the pristine black aircraft emblazoned with the Knight Inc. logo. The captain greeted Lucien warmly; wherever the destination was, it seemed to be a journey Lucien made regularly.

Inside the cabin, the aircraft was the last word in aviation luxury.

And what else would she have expected? Deep leather recliners, gleaming wooden panels and expensive fittings surrounded her, and it came as no surprise that they were the only passengers.

Lucien dispensed with his black leather jacket as soon as the doors were closed.

"Is this your jet?" Sophie asked.

Lucien shrugged. "I fly a lot."

She glanced behind her.

"Are there any cabin crew?"

"Do you want there to be?"

Sophie's brows knitted together. *Did she?* Was she content to be alone in the skies with Lucien?

"I don't think I do," she said eventually.

Lucien nodded, and waved an arm towards the seating area.

"We're going to be in the air for around five hours. Make yourself comfortable."

Five hours? That was far more than Sophie had anticipated, and worry prickled over her skin. She was flying God knows where with a man she'd only known for a few days. *What if she didn't make it home on time?*

Guilt swooped in and landed heavily on her chest. She was

thinking like a deceitful lover. Did Dan feel this way every time he met with the woman he'd decided was more worthy of his attention that she was? Did he worry about covering his tracks? She thought about it, and much as she tried to retrospectively apply guilt and remorse to Dan's behaviour, she drew a blank. *What did that tell her?* Either her husband wasn't bothered if she uncovered his infidelity, or else he genuinely believed that she was too stupid to join the dots. Neither option gave her much comfort.

"Don't worry, Cinders. You'll be home by sun-up on Sunday."

Sophie nodded and sank down into the nearest recliner, grateful once again for Lucien's perceptiveness.

She needed to think like a man, to compartmentalise her life. She could do that. She could lock her marital problems away in a sealed file marked with Sunday's date. She visualised herself closing the file and setting the seal, and then storing it away in the recesses of her head. Dan no doubt had none of these problems, but then wasn't he so much more practised in the art of deceit?

"Where are we going?" she asked, as much to fill her head with something new as from genuine curiosity.

"We're flying north." Lucien settled into the seat next to hers.

That really wasn't much help. Geography wasn't Sophie's strongest point.

"North?"

"Stop asking questions and trust me."

Sophie leaned back and closed her eyes. Being with this man was so easy, he was a born leader and she found herself more than content to follow. It was a thrill to be around someone who always knew exactly what to do.

Someone who right now had just tipped her chair back to full recline and was undoing the buttons of her filmy black chiffon blouse.

She kept her eyes closed, even though her body was screamingly awake to his touch. It was barely breakfast time, yet it seemed that Lucien was hungry for something other than bacon and eggs.

"Flying makes me horny," Lucien said as he finished her buttons and pulled her blouse out of her waistband.

Sophie bit her lip but didn't open her eyes.

"Are you sure the pilot can't see us?"

Lucien slid down the side zip of her skirt.

"If he's watching us instead of the skies, we'll know about it soon enough. There are mountains up ahead."

She lifted her hips a fraction to allow him to slide the skirt off.

Black underwear had been a necessity with her choice of blouse. The delicate, raw-edged lace of the balconette bra and high cut knickers made her feel feminine and voluptuous, and from Lucien's low, appreciative whistle, it seemed that he approved too.

Up to then she'd never had the remotest interest in joining the mile high club, but if she had, then being seduced in a private jet by a Norse love god certainly beat being ravaged in the cramped loo on Easyjet, hands down.

Sophie opened her eyes and looked into Lucien's piercing blue ones. She saw lazy lust, and could almost hear the cogs of his mind whirring as he debated what to do with her first.

So why did he have to make all the decisions, all the time?

Suddenly brave, Sophie flipped her seat back into an upright position. With satisfaction, she noted the flicker of surprise in Lucien's eyes, and then the shift from surprise to anticipation when she stood up and dropped to her knees in front of him. *What next?*

Sophie licked her lips. Lucien sat still and watched her, one eyebrow slightly raised. Nerves danced a tango in her belly.

Did she have what it took to be in control of this man at this moment, to make him feel the way he did her?

There was only one way to find out. She reached out a hand to the shirt button at the base of his throat and pushed it open. His eyebrow inched a little higher, while her fingers inched a little lower, opening the next button.

Pop, pop, pop, and suddenly he was bared to his washboard abs. Sophie sighed with satisfaction, struck all over again by how perfectly sculpted he was.

How could someone so gorgeous not be vain? Because he wasn't. He was cocksure and verging on arrogant, but he didn't use his beauty as a weapon in the way many would be tempted to. It was just there, ready to scorch the eyeballs off anyone whose gaze lingered on him for more than a few seconds. Right now, Sophie was on fire.

She grazed her nails down his hard chest, through the smattering of golden hairs all the way to the barrier of his belt buckle. *It was in her way.* She worked it open in a couple of seconds, and as soon as she released it she could feel his erection straining for release from his jeans. Knowing that she'd excited him excited her too, and she leaned in, wrapping herself around him to claim the kiss that waited for her on his lips. Slow and intensely sexual, the lingering caress of his mouth wiped out any doubts about her ability to take the lead for a while.

With a little regret, she braced her hands on his shoulders and pushed him back against his seat. He took it well. Rolling his shoulders and settling in, he lifted himself for her when she put her hands on the top of his jeans and dragged them down to his feet.

How come he was the one in the compromising position, yet she was the one who felt more exposed?

His cock rose between them, hard, proud and mouth-watering. Sophie closed her eyes for a second and swallowed, then looked into Lucien's eyes and ran her tongue over her top lip.

"Tell me what you want me to do, Lucien," she breathed. "I won't do it unless you tell me."

He reached out and tapped her nose lightly. "Touché, Ms. Black. Now stroke my cock."

A tiny smile flitted across her lips as she reached out and circled him with her fingers. He shifted in response to her hands on him and watched, mesmerised, as she brought her hands up to her lips and dampened her fingers with her own saliva. His cock was solid silk underneath the slick stroke of her hands, his balls warm and heavy as she cupped them. She flicked him one of his almost imperceptible trademark winks. She was enjoying this, the shift in power, using the skills he'd taught her to turn him on. Leaning in, she tongued his nipples then glanced down at her hands around his erection.

"Like this, Mr. Knight?" she asked, then leisurely licked her fingers again and interlocked her hands around him. *Jesus, he was hard.* She stroked his length, letting her thumbs slide over the throbbing head with every upward sweep. Lucien responded with a heavy groan and pushed his cock harder into her hands.

"Come on, Lucien," Sophie whispered, giddy with lust. "Spell it out for me."

His eyes were so dark that she could barely make out any blue, and his chest rose in tell-tale shallow rasps.

"Suck my cock, Sophie. Slide your gorgeous mouth all the way over it."

Chapter Nineteen

Sophie moistened her lips and settled her bottom on her ankles between his knees, then leaned in close and ran the tip of her tongue around the head of his cock. Holding him firmly, she took him in her mouth and swirled her tongue around him until he moaned and one of his hands snaked into her hair. Lust blazed a trail through Sophie all the way down to her sex, ignited by the thrill of kneeling in front of him and being held down.

He was a feast, and she gorged on him. Every slide and swirl of her tongue, every bob of her head pushed him closer, made him harder, until he wasn't stroking her hair so much as grasping her head in both hands and thrusting into her mouth. Sophie stepped up the co-ordinated speed of her slippery hands and her sliding mouth, feeling him hot and hard and about to burst. She glanced up the contours of his body to find him watching her, and the intimacy of the eye contact was all it took to send him over the edge. His hips juddered and salty hot semen pumped into the back of her throat, evidence of what she'd done to him. What she'd done *for* him.

She swallowed it down, his cock still throbbing in her mouth, his hands gentle now on her hair and shoulders. Sophie closed her eyes and laid her cheek against the firmness of his thigh, her lips lazy over his balls as she listened to his breathing turn slowly from ragged to steady.

"I guess that's another one you can cross off that list of yours. Or two actually," she said, drawing herself up on her knees to face him.

"Two?" His arms slid around her and pulled her close against his naked body.

"Two." She nodded for emphasis, enjoying the heat of his chest against hers. "For one, I've joined the mile high club."

His mouth twisted. "It's a tacky reference, but I'll accept it. And the second?"

"I've blown my boss." Sophie felt her cheeks flare pink as soon as the words left her mouth.

Lucien nodded. "But we still need to work on that blush."

He reached around her and unclipped her bra, then slid it off her body. "You're still blushing."

What did he expect? She was kneeling between his thighs wearing nothing but her underwear as his private jet bore her through the skies, destination unknown. This was not her average Friday morning.

"You're pink all the way from here..." - he touched his fingers to her warm cheeks - "To here." He swept his fingertips down her neck to hold her breasts in his palms like a fruit seller might cup oranges, his thumbs playing with her nipples. He ducked down to suck each one in turn, then licked her lips before sliding his tongue into her mouth.

"Stand up."

She heard his quiet command, but faltered with a fresh attack of nerves.

"Sophie..." his tone was quiet but brooked no argument. Still hot-cheeked, she got to her feet. She felt intensely exposed, standing in the cabin of the jet in just her knickers. And then she felt even more exposed when Lucien peeled them down her legs.

"Step out of them."

She lifted one foot and then the other for him to remove them over her high heels.

"And stop blushing."

"I can't," she said, and clamped her hands to her cheeks. She was completely nude and Lucien's head was level with her crotch. "You're certain the pilot won't come in?"

Lucien looked up from between her legs and ran one fingertip all the way from her perineum to the front of her sex.

"I'm certain." His finger swept back along the same path. "I couldn't swear for the co-pilot though."

Sophie gasped. "There's more than one of them through there?" She glanced towards the cockpit doorway and tried to step back, but Lucien's hands landed on her hips and held her captive.

"Lucien, I..." Sophie's protest died on her lips at the first touch of his insistent tongue. However much she feared being caught naked by the co-pilot, the wicked anticipation of what Lucien was about to do was more compelling. He scooted forward to sit on the edge of his seat, his beautiful face upturned between her spread legs. Sophie couldn't recall ever feeling more sexual than at that moment, standing in stiletto heels, naked, with her incredible lover gazing right up into her sex. And then she felt more raunchy still, as he spread her open with his fingers and stroked the tip of his tongue over her clitoris.

He looked up her body and locked eyes with her. Sophie sucked in a deep breath, beyond turned on at the sight of him buried nose deep in her sex. She jittered deliciously, not knowing where to put her hands. She'd tried them on her hips but the stance felt too contrived, flaunting herself overtly.

Flaunting overtly was about right, there was no getting away from it.

"Play with your tits," he said, close against her clitoris, and the vibrations of his voice on her flesh made her quiver. She cupped her breasts as he watched, and he rewarded her by pushing two fingers inside her and pumping them slowly.

Sophie lost any lingering inhibitions and threw her head back in abandonment as Lucien made a thorough exploration of her sex with his tongue. He fucked her with his fingers and her orgasm came inevitably hard and fast. She reached down and clutched his head to her as he relentlessly swirled his tongue over her clitoris.

His mouth stilled slowly as her fingers loosened in his hair. He looked up and inclined his head towards a door at one end of the cabin.

"Just for future reference, Princess... there's a bedroom through there."

Sophie looked at him incredulously, but he just lifted a nonchalant shoulder.

He'd deliberately placed her in a position where they might be seen rather than retire to the privacy of the bedroom.

"You could have said."

"Why? So you could hide? Be honest, Sophie. Knowing someone might walk in on us made it even hotter, didn't it?" Challenge lit his blue eyes.

Sophie bent to step into her knickers and thought about his question. 'Be honest', he'd said. Honesty was the one thing her marriage was woefully short on, so Lucien's demand of it in every aspect of his life was something she was coming to admire greatly. He was the Svengali of his own sexual honesty cult, and she was a willing handmaiden.

"Honestly?" She snapped her bra back in place as he fastened his belt. "Yes. It added something to think someone... someone in uniform... might come through and discover us." There was a thrill in just admitting it. She paused, trying to find the words to express herself. "It felt... naughtier."

He raised his eyebrows at her.

"You have a thing for uniforms then, Ms. Black?"

"What? No!" Sophie buttoned her blouse out of sequence and had to unbutton it and start again. "I just mean that I see what you mean. The possibility of being caught was... umm... sexy."

Lucien nodded. "I think you've just added a new item to the list for us to work on."

She looked up quizzically as she zipped her skirt.

Lucien shrugged his shirt back on.

"Voyeurism."

Fully dressed again, Sophie shook her head firmly.

"Wherever we're going, Lucien, I'm not having outdoor sex

while people watch."

Lucien pushed a hand through the hair she'd recently been clutching onto.

"For the record, voyeurism doesn't have to mean being outside. And anyway, I wouldn't recommend too much outdoor sex where we're headed, Princess. It's inside the Arctic Circle."

Chapter Twenty

The Arctic Circle? As in snow, and glaciers, and polar bears?

Sophie glanced down at her filmy blouse in alarm. This outfit was not going to cut it. She was going to freeze to death.

"Don't worry, you'll be fine, it's not much different to an English winter up there at the moment. You've brought a coat, yes?"

Sophie nodded, unconvinced. Her beautiful wool holly berry red coat kept her cosy enough at home, but it wouldn't be the choice of your average Eskimo.

Lucien crossed to the self-service galley and returned with a platter of croissants, pastries, cheeses and continental meats.

"Breakfast is served, madam."

Sophie looked at the array of foods and realised she was starving. Being with Lucien made her forget the most basic things, eating included. Her husband should probably be added to that list too.

"Is your life always like this?" she asked, after she'd loaded her plate. "Private jets, any woman you want, champagne on tap?"

Lucien studied her over the brim of his steaming coffee cup.

"Pretty much."

He was utterly unapologetic, but then why wouldn't he be? It was a dream lifestyle, and Google had reliably informed her that at thirty-one, Lucien Knight was the complete self-made man. His business acumen was much documented and lauded, even if his history before Knight Inc. was a blank page.

"Don't you ever want more, though?"

"More? One private jet is enough, even for me," he said dryly.

"No... I didn't mean..." - she waved an arm around the luxurious cabin - "...this. What about family? What about love... kids one day, maybe?"

Lucien blew out a breath and shook his head. "Not my bag, Princess. Ties don't do it for me."

"Everyone needs love, Lucien."

"Yeah, and Santa really exists." Lucien pushed his plate away. "Where's love got you, Sophie?"

Sophie dipped her head, stung by his words. Or stung by the truth behind his words. Love had got her precisely nowhere. Maybe he was right. He'd built a life for himself that was all about fun without heartache. What was so bad about that?

"But don't you get lonely sometimes?"

Lucien shrugged. "I own seven clubs and twenty nine retail shops around the country, and I have a staff of over five hundred, including a terribly distracting PA. I don't have time to be lonely."

Much as Sophie wanted to dig deeper, something in Lucien's face had shut down. His glittering eyes had dulled to a flat blue, and a muscle twitched along the hard set of his jaw. His answers had told her precisely nothing, and she got the distinct feeling that they had been structured to have exactly that effect. The man should be a politician. *Who are you, Lucien Knight?*

However intimate they had been over the last few days, in any way that counted, the man sitting opposite her was a complete stranger.

Lucien closed the bedroom door quietly, relieved that Sophie had accepted his suggestion that she change into jeans and try to catch up on some sleep for the rest of the flight. Her questions over breakfast had unsettled him. He wasn't lonely, and the last thing on his agenda was being shackled to someone else.

Why did anyone ever think monogamy was going to work? It wasn't natural. People were sexual beings, marriage artificially suppressed nature's desires. It warped those who tried to conform to the rules, and made villains and victims out of those who failed.

Sophie's marriage was a case in point. Her husband was half way around the world enjoying the carnal pleasures of another woman's body, while his wife lay in bed recovering from her latest orgasm en route to the Arctic Circle. Where was the honesty there? Where was the love, and the much fabled respect?

Lucien glanced towards the bedroom door. He was determined that Sophie would enjoy far more carnal pleasures before she went home and into battle with her cheating husband.

Daniel Black was a worried man. He couldn't get hold of his wife. He could hardly make a scene about it with Maria, but Sophie's silence could only mean one thing. He wasn't a dramatic man, it didn't occur to him that anything untoward might have happened to her. Gut instinct told him that Sophie was choosing to avoid his calls. Cold fear wrapped clammy fingers around his heart at the thought that she knew about his affair.

Never in a million years did he entertain the idea that Sophie herself might be too busy in the arms of another man to listen to his ever more desperate pleas for her to pick up his messages.

Back in suburbia, their ordinary little semi stood neglected, the flashing red of the answering machine the only light in the place.

Red for hazard. Red for danger. Red for trouble ahead.

Chapter Twenty-One

"Are you sure I'm not going to die of hypothermia?"

Sophie cast an anxious glance at Lucien as the jet taxied to a halt on the small runway. Lucien had yet to elaborate on exactly where they were, but by the looks of the dramatic, snow-peaked landscape they'd flown over, they were somewhere extremely cold.

Lucien wound a soft black woollen scarf that smelt deliciously of him around her neck, having reached it down from an overhead locker.

"You'll be fine." He cast a doubtful look at her feet. "Your shoes wouldn't be most people's choice for the Arctic Circle, but you'll be fine."

He pulled his leather jacket on and opened the aircraft doors with the ease of someone who did it often. "Welcome to Norway, Ms. Black. Mind your step."

He paused momentarily at the top of the steps, inhaled deeply, then headed down onto the tarmac with his head bowed. Sophie followed, relieved to feel the cool but by no means freezing wind on her cheeks as she breathed in the fresh crystal air.

Norway. Once again, Lucien had managed to do the last thing she'd expected. Any other playboy might have chosen Paris, or perhaps Venice. Not Lucien. For some unfathomable reason, he'd decided that the Arctic Circle was the appropriate setting for seduction.

He hustled her straight into the warm leather interior of a waiting limousine, and within seconds they were easing out of the small airport and onto the open road.

Sophie watched in wonder out of the window, exhilarated by her first glimpse of Norway. Snow-peaked mountains reared up into pale blue skies, fringed all around with lush early autumn greens and golds. It looked like a scene out of a picture book, too perfect to be real.

"It's breathtaking," she breathed, as much to herself as Lucien.

"Those are the Lyngen Alps." Lucien gestured out of the window at the majestic mountains. "We're up in the very north of the country, high above the Arctic Circle."

"It's very beautiful." Sophie murmured. "I feel like Maria from The Sound of Music."

"Wrong country – that's Austria," he corrected her, and slid an arm around her shoulders and pulled her against him in the plush rear seat of the car. "You can dress up as a governess if you like though. Or a nun."

Sophie rolled her eyes. "Do you ever *not* think about sex?"

"Where's the fun in that?"

Sophie looked back out at the beautiful scenery. He'd been joking, but she envied Lucien his outlook. He worked hard, played hard, and he never had his heart broken. As far as she knew, anyway. Wasn't that a better plan than most people's? Do a job you hate, watch too much TV, and lay yourself open to the devastation of love and loss?

"Do you come here often?" As soon as the words left Sophie's lips, she regretted them. She'd intended to ask a genuine question and managed to make it sound like a come-on. But Lucien didn't pull her up on the innuendo.

"Less often than I'd like." It was his turn to gaze out of the window. Sophie frowned, unsure what she'd said to make him close off. From the way he'd clammed up in the jet earlier and the way his face had hardened just now, she could tell that he didn't appreciate these kind of questions. What did he mean, not as often as he'd like? Did he have personal obligations here?

"Do you have clubs in Norway?"

"No."

Lucien pressed a button and the privacy glass between the driver and the rear of the limo slid into place.

"Stop asking questions and get over here." He pulled her onto his lap and glanced at his watch. "We have approximately fourteen minutes." His hand slid along her thigh. "I bet I can make you come within three."

Exactly fourteen minutes later the limo eased to a stop, and Sophie straightened her blouse before the driver opened her door. She stepped outside and stood beside Lucien, still throbbing from his ministrations.

Wow. They'd pulled into the driveway of a gorgeous, low-slung wooden lodge, the mother of all log cabins. The undulating timber facade and white-washed window frames were in perfect harmony with the surroundings, all the way up to the slopes of its grass-covered roof. It looked organic, as if it had grown from the earth around it rather than been crafted by man.

But however beautiful the building was, it paled in comparison with the scenery that surrounded it. Set on the shores of a glittering fjord, whose waters reflected the pale sunlight, the house stood against a backdrop of soaring granite mountains, their tips blanketed with snow. The whole vista exuded Nordic health and understated wealth, a luxury, boutique getaway for those lucky enough to be able to afford it.

Sophie scanned around for other people. There were none.

"Is it a hotel?" she asked, doubtfully.

"No. It's mine."

"Yours?" It shouldn't have come as a surprise, but it did. Lucien was such an urbanite; it seemed at odds with his lifestyle that he should choose to own a home here amongst these pristine, quiet mountains. Sophie realised she'd had the same kind of thought when she'd first seen his UK home. He refused to conform to easy stereotypes, she reflected, and he was all the more unreadable for it.

The car slunk away as Lucien led her through the main door directly into the living area of an airy, open plan lodge. Sophie slowed to a halt, drinking in the way nature blended with luxury to create a space just as breathtaking as Lucien's other home. It was very different, and yet it had similar nuances of clean style and elegance that made it uniquely, subtly, and totally Lucien Knight.

Soft wood juxtaposed with exposed stone complemented the soft white walls. Uncluttered but never stark, cool but not cold. One side of the sunken lounge area was almost entirely made up of glass; huge picture windows paid appropriate homage to the glorious views beyond. Sophie found herself drawn towards it, struck by the ambient warmth inside compared to the crisp freshness outside, as she laid a palm against the glass.

"You've surprised me," she said, and turned to face him.

Lucien rested his arm on the mantel of the massive stone fireplace. "Why so?"

"This place... the Arctic Circle... it's so, umm..." Sophie paused as she fished around for the right phrase. "So, well, unexpectedly wholesome," she finished eventually.

"I see." Lucien reached into the pocket of his leather jacket. "Wholesome."

He placed the object from his pocket in the centre of the wooden mantel and turned back to watch Sophie suck in a surprised breath. Sunlight glinted off the silver, acorn-shaped butt plug.

"Before nightfall, Ms. Black," Lucien promised. "You're blushing again." He sauntered over and admonished her with a tap on the end of her nose. "Let me show you around."

Notes of pride slid into his tone as he gave her the guided tour, and Sophie could well see why. The whole place had been engineered around the stunning mountain views, and each room flowed organically into the next. Dove-grey flagstones lined the floors underfoot, and soft suede fabrics and fur throws added warm, welcoming touches to sofas that begged to be lounged on. The whole place exuded comfort and warmth, and Sophie found herself utterly enchanted.

"Lunch?"

The normality of Lucien's question caught her unaware. It was disorienting to shift constantly from the plane of near-fantasy - this movie-star lifestyle, the ever-present undercurrents of desire - back to ordinary reality, but on reflection she found she was more than ready to eat.

He led her back through to the dining room, which on previous inspection had been empty. Not any more. An older woman dressed smartly in an understated black trouser suit looked up and smiled warmly at Lucien as she put the finishing touches to the feast she'd laid out on the dining table.

"Everything is ready for you, Mr. Knight." She spoke in lightly accented English and inclined her head towards Sophie to include her in the conversation. "Enjoy."

And they did. Sophie was blown away by the array of fresh seafood, some warm and some cold, all served with dips and bread. It was delicious, and she sampled a little of everything as Lucien explained how he'd had the lodge designed and built five years back.

"Why here?" she asked, as he topped up her wine glass with crisp, chilled Chablis. "Why Norway? It seems such an unusual choice."

"Where would you expect?"

Sophie shrugged. "I don't know. If I could choose anywhere, I'd probably go for somewhere with sunshine."

"We have sunshine in Norway." Lucien gestured towards the window and the undeniable gleam of sunlight off the fjord.

"We?"

Lucien paused momentarily. "We. They. What difference does it make?"

"Nothing, really... you just sounded... territorial."

Lucien swirled his wine around in his glass, and his downward glance felt like the curtain falling on the conversation. It was too late though. Sophie suddenly knew exactly why here, why Norway. This was more than a holiday home for Lucien. This was his homeland.

Lucien glanced at her empty plate and finished his wine. "Come on. I'll show you outside."

Sophie snuggled deeper into her coat, Lucien's black scarf wrapped around her neck as he took her hand and led her around the outside of the cabin. She was utterly smitten with the majesty of the mountains, and breathed in deeply to fill her lungs with invigorating air. Her earlier realisation about Lucien's heritage seemed so obvious in retrospect, he looked every inch a proud Norwegian now she'd made the connection.

He was the most enigmatic man she'd ever met. On the one hand he was a Thor-like sex warrior, perfectly at home slinking around the debaucherous outposts of his commercial empire, and on the other hand he was a man who craved his solitude and privacy and loved this rare and extra-ordinary setting. It was a heady combination, and it left Sophie wanting very much to know the roots of this man who existed between the two extremes.

"And this is the jacuzzi."

Lucien's words broke her reverie, and she refocused on the wrap-around deck that surrounded the cabin. They were at the back of the lodge now, facing directly out over the lake and distant mountains. A large, steaming hot tub squatted square in front of her, and a smile of pure bliss touched her lips at the idea of climbing into the warm bubbles and looking out at that view. Lucien splayed his hands to the side, obviously especially proud of this extra special touch.

"Fancy a dip?" she asked, saucily echoing the question he'd asked her back in the Gateway Club.

"Maybe later."

"Touché."

Sophie trailed her fingers in the warm water.

"I can't anyway. I didn't bring a bikini."

Lucien rolled his eyes. "As if I'd let you wear one." He pressed a button and the jacuzzi stopped bubbling. "Until tonight." The sudden silence on the deck was deafening. "Let's go inside." Lucien took her still damp hand in his own warm one. "There's something we need to do."

Chapter Twenty-Two

Back in the lounge, Sophie was gladdened to see the freshly laid fire crackling in the fireplace. The air outside held a wintry nip, and she kicked off her shoes and moved to stand in front of the flames to warm her bottom. Lucien shrugged out of his jacket and crossed to stand in front of her to unwind her scarf, then unbuttoned her coat and eased it down her arms. Despite the loss of a layer, Sophie felt warmer rather than chilled, a combination of the effect of the fire and the heat of desire that always found her when she looked at this man.

"The staff have all gone home." He stroked a fingertip over her collarbone.

The meaning behind his words was clear. *We're alone here, we can do whatever we like.* The fire that warmed her backside was nothing to the blaze his words sparked in her belly. Lucien's eyes slid over her shoulder, and without turning around she knew what he was looking at. The acorn. His eyes moved back to hers, a glint of amusement in them as he ran a hand behind her and fondled her bottom.

"Now strip off and bend over."

Sophie's eyes widened in alarm, but Lucien shook his head.

"I'm joking, Sophie." His hand still stroked her denim-clad backside. "Haven't you learned yet to trust me?" His other hand moved to play with the top button of her blouse. "By the time we get around to using that acorn, you'll be begging for it."

Sophie's gaze lingered on his mouth. She didn't doubt him for a second. His lips parted a little, and she leaned in close. Nose to nose, breath to breath, until she watched his eyelids drift down a second before his mouth touched hers.

Desire coursed through her as he took his own sweet time with the kiss, his hands stroking her body as his tongue danced a slow tango with hers. Sophie felt her nipples peak as his palms brushed her breasts, and she reached for her buttons to remove the barriers of clothing. She wanted his hands on her skin.

"Too warm, Ms. Black?"

Lucien helped her off with her blouse and shed his shirt too, then paused to run a finger down the strap of her lace bra. "Shall I take this off too?" Sophie got the distinct impression that the question did not require much of an answer, but she played along.

"I am still rather hot," she supplied, and all but batted her eyelids.

Lucien unsnapped it in one assured flick.

"Better?" He slid the straps down her arms, leaving her naked from the waist up.

"I've decided you can keep the blushing," Lucien said. "You're more like a ripe peach than ever. Creamy flesh..." his fingers drifted down her throat and arrived at her nipple. "And rose pink just here." He circled his thumb around it. "And here." His other hand touched her other nipple, and he played with them delicately.

Sophie watched him, getting a kick out of the carnal pleasure in his eyes as he looked at her body. And then her eyes roved down the cords of his neck, over the beautiful definition of his shoulders and the granite contours of his abdominal muscles, and it was her turn to be seduced. He was eye-wateringly sexy, and her fingers found the top button of his jeans all of their own accord.

She flicked her eyes back to his face and saw him appraise the situation, then he reached for her jeans and mirrored her action.

She freed his second metal stud from its buttonhole, and Lucien did the same with the slightest flick of his eyebrows.

When she popped the third she knew what to expect, and seconds later they helped each other out of their jeans. Lucien went the whole way and shed his underwear at the same time, and even though she'd seen it before, Sophie swallowed hard at the sight of his cock. He was rigid and ready, as she'd known he would be. Was he ever anything else?

She left only her little black knickers on, as much for the thrill of having Lucien remove them as out of modesty.

"Do you need a little help with these?" Lucien's thumbs slid under the sides of them.

Sophie nodded and chewed her lip.

"I think I might."

He ran his hands over the material, smooth over her bottom, exploring between her legs. Sophie closed her eyes and willed him to take them off, yet he seemed in no hurry. Her eyes flew open in surprise when he placed one arm behind her knees and the other behind her back and swept her off her feet into his arms. It was so entirely primeval, and so entirely sexy to find herself held against his chest, that she looped her arms around his neck and clung on.

He held her as if she weighed nothing but air, and for a second she felt every inch the damsel in distress being rescued from disaster or the jaws of a dragon. *Except no disaster movie she'd ever seen featured the hero stark naked with the head of his erection skimming the damsel's backside.*

His mouth was a temptation, right there and ripe when she tilted her face up. She tightened her arms around his neck and pulled his kiss to her, a gentle, slow graze of his mouth that left her wanting, a languid hint of tongue that sent her reeling. Her fingers crept into his hair and held his mouth to hers, and she shifted in his arms to feel his cock rub against her bottom a little more. It was a prelude, and already he had her gagging for the main event.

He eased down onto his knees and laid her on the huge sheepskin rug in front of the fireplace. She wriggled her back against the soft sensation.

Lucien turned briefly to the large coffee table and opened the drawer underneath to extract something. When he turned back, Sophie saw it was a little bottle.

"Turn over."

She sat up, then paused, as his cock was right there and irresistible. She dipped her head and licked him, then slid her mouth over him and took his length into her mouth. He groaned in appreciation, rocked his hips and stroked a hand over her hair. She felt him grow harder still, and then he wound her hair around his fingers and eased her head off him.

"Not yet, Princess." He leaned down and kissed her disappointment away, then released her hair down her back. "Lie down and turn over."

Sophie dropped back onto the rug and flipped over onto her front, her hands a pillow beneath her forehead and the heat of anticipation between her legs. Lucien brushed a fleeting kiss against the small of her back, then moved to straddle her thighs. As he settled, the tip of his erection nudged against her silk-covered backside, a reminder of what was to come.

Droplets of massage oil dripped one, two, three, down her spine, and then the same drip, drip, drip was over her shoulder blades. The lush scent of orange blossom tinged the air as Lucien placed the small glass bottle on the floor near to her face, and Sophie's eyes wandered over the black label. Neroli Sensual Massage Oil. The now familiar silver Knight Inc. logo was discreetly imprinted across the bottom, a tiny shining star over the 'i' in the name.

In *his* name. Lucien Knight, the man behind the logo, and at that moment the man behind Sophie. His hands swept down her back, making long, sure strokes to work the oil across her skin. He was feather light across her shoulders, and his thumbs rolled in rhythm up each bump of her spine, then back down again one by one to the top of her knickers. He hitched them down so they lay across the tops of her thighs, and Sophie instinctively wiggled her bared bottom. The act of having her flesh exposed felt far more indecent than simply being naked.

Lucien's warm, slippery palms closed over her buttocks and squeezed, his thumbs sinful as they slid inside the seam with every new contraction of his fingers. Each time he passed over the tight little entrance he paused for a breath, and Sophie held hers. Each time he moved on she released the breath, for the most part in relief, and a tiny part in regret. The knowledge sat between them that he intended to use the butt plug at some point before nightfall and it had her on edge, waiting, half anxious, half excited. He applied a tiny amount of pressure with his thumb on the next pass, and she tensed, gasped a little. In response Lucien leaned his head down and nuzzled her neck, his breath a warm tickle against her ear.

"Relax, Sophie." His chest blanketed her back, his hand still on her bottom. The fire had her warm all over, and his body was slick on hers thanks to the neroli oil. "It's not time yet." His thumb traced slow, secret circles as his teeth grazed her ear. "But you like this, don't you?"

Sophie closed her eyes, breathed in deeply through her nose, and nodded. She did. She really, really did.

"Good." She heard rather than saw his smile. He shifted his hand a little, replacing his thumb with his index finger. Sophie moved against his hand. The flat of his thumb had felt sensual. The pad of his crooked index finger felt predatory as he stroked her, his touch more purposeful. "You've tensed again." He kissed the nape of her neck. "Remember back to the club, Sophie. In the cinema?"

Sophie remembered it in glorious technicolour, and yes, she remembered how his finger inside her backside had made her come. But this was different. That had been quick and dirty. This was slow and sensual, and the anticipation of the silver acorn had her gasping as Lucien pushed his finger just inside her, a gentle preamble. His lips trailed her shoulder as he slid his finger out again, and then in a little bit further second time around.

He had her, and he knew it. She felt him laugh softly against her neck when she pushed her bottom upwards, an instinctive attempt to make herself more available to his touch. He gave her what she craved, pushed deeper into her and crooked his finger a little.

"You have no idea how much I'd like to fuck you here," he whispered, his mouth hot on her neck.

If he had sheathed himself and done exactly that, Sophie wouldn't have stopped him. His fingers were magic, and she was under his spell completely.

But he didn't. He eased his finger out instead and sat up.

"Turn over."

He pulled her knickers down her legs and flung them aside, then straddled her thighs again.

Sophie sucked in warm air as she looked up at him, big and bronze in the golden firelight. His thighs held hers closed, and his erection rested against her hip. His eyes moved over her and lingered on her breasts.

"You're very beautiful."

Compliments were thin on the ground in her everyday life, and Sophie usually found them hard to accept, but in that moment she had no doubt about Lucien's sincerity. His eyes told her anyway, without the need for words.

He tipped a little more neroli oil into his hands and rubbed them together, then cupped his hands over her shoulders and massaged them lightly. His erection pressed against her stomach as he leaned forward, and Sophie sighed with pleasure. It was beyond sensual, being naked and warm here with his oiled hands on her body. He took his time, sliding his hands down the lengths of her arms, transferring the oil all the way to her fingertips. Her fingers curled around his, and he squeezed them lightly before moving his hands to span her ribcage.

Sophie closed her eyes and let her emotions wash over her. Peace. Desire. Gratitude. Passion. Contentment.

And then Lucien's hands moved down to massage the apex at

the top of her legs, and the only emotion there was room for was desire.

Lucien cupped her sex and worked an oiled finger inside her lips.

Jesus, she felt good. Hot, and wet for him already. Sophie seemed to have no idea just how sexy she was, especially times like this when she gave up her inhibitions and just let go. Her body gleamed in the golden light from the fire and her clitoris blossomed as he ran his finger down the length of her sex. Her breath quickened to shallow, as did his when she sunk her teeth into the side of her hand to stop herself from crying out. He leaned in and sucked her candy pink nipples in turn, gratified by the way her fingers delved into his hair and raked his scalp. He leaned back again, one hand still between her legs, the softness of her breast in the other. Watching her give in to her body's desires was just about the sexiest thing he'd ever seen, far better than porn made for the purpose. She was all curves and softness, and every time he touched her clitoris her thighs pressed against his as she tried to open her legs.

He could so easily let her come right now, but he didn't. His eyes slid from Sophie to the silver acorn on the mantel. The next time Sophie orgasmed, it would be nestled in her bottom.

Chapter Twenty-Three

Sophie opened her eyes when Lucien eased his hands and his weight off her. *Come back!* Her body thrummed, right on the edge of orgasm, desperate for him.

He stood up. From her vantage point on the floor, he looked huge towering over her. She pushed herself up on her elbows, and reached for his hand when he held it out to pull her up. If he wanted her to stand up, she had no objections. If he'd told her to do five laps of the building naked, she would have done, utterly in his thrall now. But that was clearly not what he had in mind, so instead, she wrapped her arm around his waist and circled his cock with her other hand, her head laid against his chest as he reached for the silver acorn. He braced his arm against the mantel as she stroked his shaft, her hands still slick with oil he'd massaged into them. His heart hammered faster against her ear, and she turned her face into him and mouthed his nipple.

His arms folded around her, and this time when he lifted her off the ground his hands cupped her bottom, and she could feel the cold steel base of the butt plug against her cheek. There was no room for fear, white hot desire eclipsed it. She wrapped her legs around his waist and her arms around his neck, and Lucien held her close and kissed her deeply. Sophie opened her mouth to his tongue, lost in the intensity of being held, of being adored.

He carried her across the room and sat down on a straight backed wooden chair by the windows.

"Tell me you have a condom in your hand," she whispered,

and rocked her body against his hard cock. "I want you inside me."

Lucien opened his hand to show her the items he'd collected from the mantelpiece. A condom, a little pump of lube, and the silver butt plug.

"Wrap your legs around the chair. I want to touch your beautiful arse."

Sophie's lust spiralled as she obeyed his softly spoken demand, the wooden struts of the chair hard anchors against the back of her knees.

She was spread for him, and he pumped a little lube on his fingers and placed the things in his hands on the low ledge behind him.

His eyes locked on hers. "I'm going to touch you everywhere."

His hands moved down her body. They lingered on her breasts, brushed her stomach, and then settled beneath her spread sex, one arm behind her, one in front as she rested over his thighs. For a few long seconds he held perfectly still, and Sophie stopped breathing. She couldn't get her breath out past the heavy weight of anticipation.

He made her wait with his eyes and his body, and then his fingers all touched her at once. It was a sensory assault. Firm, massaging, sliding in and out and up and down, slippery with lube and Sophie's juices. She dug her fingernails into his shoulders and leaned her forehead against his, her eyes on his cock as he pushed two fingers inside her. His other hand smoothed up and down the crevice of her bottom, massaging lube over her tender skin.

He was beyond good at this stuff. He'd taken her from feeling fearful to wanting him to push his finger in, to wanting to know how good that silver acorn was going to feel. She reached down onto the ledge and pumped lube onto her own fingers. He'd played it so cool, so in control. She wanted to push him a little, to give something back for the riot of feelings he'd unleashed in her.

When she closed her hand around his firm cock he dragged air down sharply into his chest, and at the same time he pushed his finger deeper into her bottom. His hands were everywhere, filling her up as she pumped his lube-slippery shaft. *Jesus, she wanted him inside her.*

He tipped his head back in pure pleasure for a second, and the cords of his neck glistened with a sheen of sweat. *Christ.* He was her perfect Diet Coke man, and she couldn't resist leaning in and licking the hollow at the base of his neck. She felt rather than heard the low rumble in his throat, then he tipped his head down and kissed her, his tongue hot and searching in her mouth.

"Pass it to me, Princess." She had no need to ask what he meant. His finger still slipped slowly in and out of her bottom as she reached for it. "And the lube."

The acorn was heavy and cool in her hand. She raised her eyes to his, unsure what to do next and utterly distracted by his gentle fingers in her bottom.

"Lube it in your hands." They both looked down as she followed his instructions. "Slide your fingers around it." He eased his hand from between their bodies and covered her slippery fingers with his own. "Make it warm."

Sophie's heart beat hard against her breastbone. The silver acorn slid around in their hands as he took it from her, and he kissed her mouth slowly and moved his hand away from her bottom to gather her against him, skin to skin. His tenderness melted away any lingering echoes of anxiety, and when he touched the solid tip of the acorn against her bottom... she was ready.

Chapter Twenty-Four

Lucien held Sophie in his arms and willed himself to go slowly, to give her the very best of this new experience. She'd handed him her trust, and unlike her fuckwitted husband, he wasn't going to break it.

Her skin was warm silk in his hands, and her tongue stroked over his. She was so much more bold now, and her burgeoning courage moved him in a way very few things ever had. He could feel the tremble in her body as he touched the tip of the acorn against her bottom. She was slick with lube and her own excitement, he knew the acorn would slide inside her if she just relaxed and let it in.

"I wish it was my cock right here," he said as he worked the tip of the acorn inside her. She tensed, and then slowly relaxed her muscles. "That's it, Princess... let it in..."

Sophie's eyebrows furrowed over her squeezed shut eyes, and her teeth sank into her bottom lip. He nuzzled the tender spot beneath her ear, giving her time to get used to the new sensation.

"More?"

She rolled her hips gently and nodded, and he touched his lips against her eyelids as he pushed the acorn deeper inside.

When she took the widest part her she cried out, and he gentled her with his mouth over hers. "Feel it Sophie, full and solid inside you." She was panting, and he was finding it almost as hard to breathe himself. His cock strained to be buried inside her, but this moment was all for her, not him.

Sophie opened her eyes wide and stared into Lucien's, the butt plug buried to its flared ends in her bottom. She wanted to say something, to tell him how intense the acorn felt nestled inside her, but she couldn't find the words. She felt full, and filthy, and euphoric. Lucien's hands curled around her waist.

"Stand up."

His hands urged her up, so she stood. He did the same and fondled her bottom.

"This feels fucking amazing," he said, as he rocked the curved metal end of the butt plug. Sophie gasped and arched into the additional pressure. He was right. It felt even more amazing for her.

"Now sit on the chair."

She looked down at the hard wooden seat of the chair, then uncertainly back up at Lucien.

Trust me, he'd said. She closed her eyes as her bottom made contact with the unyielding chair, and the pressure inside her increased ten fold as the plug pushed against her vagina. Lucien dropped onto his knees and parted her legs, and then, with a speed that took her breath away, he ducked down and sucked her clitoris into his mouth. He swirled his tongue over her, and Sophie gasped and pushed her feet down hard onto the floor in erotic shock as a sudden and intense orgasm ricocheted through her body.

"Oh Jesus... Lucien..." Sophie clutched his shoulders as her muscles contracted. Her entire body throbbed, and her muscles tightened deliciously around the acorn. Every sensation was magnified. Every wave of her orgasm became more intense with the new fullness.

He slid up her body and kissed her hard, the taste of her sex on his lips, her body still pulsing with pleasure. She reached down behind her on the ledge for the condom, crazy with need for him.

"Fuck me, Lucien."

He took the silver foil from her fingers, his eyes blue-black with lust.

"Get on your knees, Sophie. I want to look at your beautiful arse when I screw you."

Sophie dissolved into him as he pulled her down to the floor. Lucien had tapped deep into the essence of her womanhood in a way Dan had never dug deep enough to discover. He made her feel more intensely female than ever before, more sexy, more aware of what she wanted and of what she had to give.

He wanted her from behind. She wanted him to take her from behind. But she wanted it her way, and she felt confident enough to take the reins for a moment, certain that he'd be even more turned on if she did. She was on all fours, and as she crawled the few feet to the grey velvet couch, the butt plug moved inside her, a filthy thrill that caught her by surprise and made her gasp. When she reached the sofa she turned and threw a wantonly inviting glance over her shoulder at Lucien, then turned back to rest her elbows on the sofa and rounded her bottom provocatively out at him.

"That's a mighty fine view, Ms.Black."

He was behind her and kissing the cheeks of her ass in seconds, his mouth hot and his tongue wet as it trailed around the butt plug. Sophie sucked in air as she heard the tell-tale rip of foil, and his fingers moved forwards to caress between her legs. *Yes, God, yes.* She was open and desperate for him, and she cried out with pleasure when he finally pushed himself inside her. Slow and easy, he instinctively took his time as he introduced her to yet another new experience, and any lingering fear melted away as the incredible sensations took over. *Jesus.* He pulled back slowly, and then rocked into her until his hips touched her body. He was so deep inside that she could feel his cock push against the butt plug. Ecstasy had her trembling, instantly on the edge of coming again, closer with every satisfying thud of Lucien's body into hers.

His fingers were everywhere... putting gentle pressure on the plug in rhythm with each plunge of his cock... stroking her clitoris, making her whimper with the need for release... tightening in her hair as he neared orgasm himself and banged her harder, faster. Sophie's orgasm began in her fingertips and toes, violent volts of pleasure so intense that she physically jolted and screamed out as it engulfed her. Lucien wound her hair around his hand and pulled her head back, and she slammed herself harder onto his pumping cock until his orgasm ripped out of him; long, pulsating and powerful.

Sophie sagged down onto the sofa, exhausted, Lucien's hands gentle now on her hips. He eased out of her as her breathing slowed, then pulled her up with him onto the pillowy depths of the sofa. She was boneless, spent - half way to sleep already, as he tucked her into the crook of his arm and tugged a fur throw off the back of the sofa to nestle around them. It was utter bliss. She sank into the warm circle of his arms and closed her eyes.

Chapter Twenty-Five

Darkness had fallen when Sophie opened her eyes again, and firelight filled the room with dancing golden shadows. She was incredibly comfortable, cocooned in fur, and a small but delicious stretch confirmed that the acorn was still tucked inside her. *Where was Lucien?* She propped herself up on one elbow and glanced around the empty room. Their clothes were still on the floor, and the little glass bottle of neroli oil sat on the coffee table. A crumb trail to the most sensational sex of her life, right there.

The door opened and Lucien appeared with two steaming mugs in his hands.

"I was just about to wake you. Do you always sleep so soundly after sex?"

Sophie pulled herself up to sitting and tucked the blanket underneath her armpits. The hot mug Lucien handed her was topped with cream and chocolate shavings, and delicious wafts of alcohol-laced hot chocolate filled her nostrils.

"You exhausted me." She dipped her finger into the cream and sucked it.

"Naturally," Lucien shrugged.

He was wearing his battered jeans and nothing else, and Sophie admired the way the firelight enhanced the lean muscles across his shoulders.

Why her? He was a man who could take his pick, so quite why he had zeroed in on her was a mystery she wasn't brave enough to try to solve. *Was it just that she had wandered into his main beam?* The idea that whoever had landed the job as his PA would be here right now flitted into her mind, but she dismissed it. Whatever else Lucien might be, he didn't seem the kind of guy to just fuck for the sake of it. For pleasure, certainly, but just because there was a woman around him whom he hadn't had yet? *No.* She wasn't harbouring romantic hopes or feelings of love, but they had an undeniable connection that was more than just physical.

Sex with Lucien was... immersion. She felt saturated in him, drenched to the skin with lust whenever he touched her. He was touching her now, massaging her ankle as he sat down on the end of the sofa with his mug in his hand. Sophie sipped her steaming chocolate and watched the fire.

When his hand moved a little higher to rub her calf muscle, she stretched her leg out onto his lap.

"Thank you," she said, softly.

Lucien turned to study her.

"For what?"

She inclined her head, encompassing the room, the moment, the setting beyond the dark windows.

"For this. For here."

Lucien stroked the tender skin at the back of her knee.

"It's my pleasure. And yours too, if I'm not mistaken."

She sipped her chocolate, the brandy in it strong and fortifying.

"I've never known pleasure like this."

"Good." He nodded. "As it should be." His eyes didn't meet hers as he massaged her knee absently, and for a few quiet minutes he seemed a world away. "Drink up. There's something you should see."

Sophie stood on the deck overlooking the fjord, her head tipped back to the skies in wonder. Wrapped in the fur blanket to protect her from the cold air, the only thing she noticed was the astral majesty overhead.

The dark night sky was alive with magical streaks of colour. Ethereal white wisps sprinkled with pink glitter swirled around luminous green ghost dancers, great streaks of light that bubbled and rolled as if being stirred from above by an invisible witch. It was easily the most stunning thing Sophie had ever seen.

"Wow," she whispered. It was inadequate, but the sight left her almost speechless. "Wow."

"Pretty special, huh?"

Sophie wanted to answer him, but found she couldn't. Standing there beneath nature's glorious slideshow, words failed her. This world was so far from her own, a bigger, better place where unfaithful husbands and broken marriages didn't matter. These vast, rolling skies reached out and touched her heart, performing their graceful dance just for her. She didn't realise that there were tears on her face until she tasted salt on her lips. Finally, she turned to Lucien behind her.

"Is it always like this?"

He shook his head. "This is quite early in the year for us. The nights are drawing in fast here now, we only see the Aurora in the colder months."

Sophie looked up again, eager to see more, then looked back down as a whirring noise started up behind her. The previously still waters of the jacuzzi had fizzed into life, the warm, steaming bubbles lit by underwater illuminations reminiscent of the skies above. Lucien stood beside it, a bottle of champagne and two glasses in his spread hands.

It was an invitation that no woman could refuse. A beautiful man, and a warm jacuzzi beneath skies painted with an ever-changing palette by Mother Nature's paintbrush. Already bathed in a heady sense of liberation, Sophie let the fur blanket fall to the floor and walked across the deck towards him.

Lucien watched Sophie cross towards him, naked and free, perfectly framed by the mountains and the neon-flashed skies behind her. She reminded him of a mystical nymph, as if she'd just walked out of the waters of the fjord and onto his deck. A living fantasy.

She had no inkling of how glorious she was - and how much more so now that she had shaken off the grey shroud of unhappiness that she'd worn around her shoulders like an invisible cloak the first time she'd walked into his office.

He had her for one more day, and he was going to make every second count.

Sophie sank into the heavenly bubbles as Lucien stripped off his jeans. He looked so perfectly at home in the nude, it was his default setting. She settled onto the dipped seat beneath the water, reminded again of the butt plug's presence as it moved a little deeper inside her. She fidgeted, enjoying the dark new sensation of fullness, the way it pressed against the back of her vagina. It was no-hands foreplay, made all the more sexy by the fact that the look in Lucien's perceptive eyes told her that he knew exactly what she was feeling. As the tingle of sexual excitement began again, Sophie marvelled at how her body continually craved more of this man. He made her insatiable.

"So, tell me. What do you think of the acorn?"

His fingers slid lightly over the back of Sophie's neck as he settled into the warmth of the water alongside her.

Sophie wriggled in her seat, hyper-aware of his touch and the warm jets of water bubbling underneath her. When she moved, it sprayed directly between her thighs, and she couldn't help but spread her legs a little. It felt so damn good, like a secret, intimate massage. She moved again and the water pummelled her clitoris. Lucien licked her ear, his fingers playing idly with her stiff nipples.

His open mouth slid down her neck. "Just let it happen."

Sophie closed her eyes as Lucien stretched behind her and powered up the intensity of the jets. *Jesus.* The anticipation of her climax tightened her body. She dropped her head back on Lucien's arm, enjoying his hands over her breasts as she built towards the release only an orgasm could give her.

She rocked her body in the seat, restlessly searching for enough intensity to push her over the edge. The butt plug moved inside her, a sexy fullness that was all the more delicious for still being unfamiliar.

Lucien met her gaze and held it, then ran his tongue over his slightly parted lips. It was all it took. Sophie moaned softly as she came hard and fast, ecstasy all the more intense for sharing it eye to eye with Lucien. He moved in close and kissed her, slow and open mouthed as her body softened from taut to relaxed in his arms.

Sophie closed her eyes and surrendered to the sensations. The ripples and bubbles of the warm water. The stroke of Lucien's tongue in her mouth, and the rhythmic pressure of his thumb, back and forth over her ribcage. The feeling of her hammering heart slowing in her chest as her body settled against his. The kaleidoscope skies that would be there when she opened her eyes and looked up. It was a fairy tale, albeit a very grown up one. A fantasy, maybe. Not real life, anyway. Sophie couldn't imagine how her old life could possibly still be waiting for her in the UK, a comfortable pair of slippers compared to the sexy stiletto lifestyle she'd led at Lucien's side this past week.

Much as she didn't want them to, the bony fingers of reality poked at her, sharp digs that made her sigh heavily. She opened her eyes and found him watching her.

"What am I doing here, Lucien? I don't recognise my own life any more."

"Is that a bad thing?"

Sophie twisted her damp hair into a rope over one shoulder. "This week has been…" She cast around for the words to sum up what a cataclysmic shift the past week had been for her. "It's been amazing, but I have to go home and face reality on Sunday."

Lucien twirled the coil of her hair around his own hand.

"You do. But at least you know that there are other options now."

"Are there, really?" She searched his open expression for answers. "How can I carry on working for you after this?" She gazed around at the celestial beauty overhead, and the shadowy mountain ranges. "This is your world, Lucien. It's real to you. For me, it's a one week fantasy."

"Only if you want it to be. I still need a PA, Sophie, and you're shaping up to be pretty good at it."

"I've barely done any work," she pointed out softly.

"On the contrary. You've exceeded my expectations by quite some way." Lucien's eyes glinted with amusement at her as he uncorked the champagne and poured it.

"Was this always your plan?" she asked. "Did you employ me because you saw me as a bored wife ready to stray?"

He laughed low in his throat and laid his head back on the ledge of the jacuzzi, his eyes on the moving skies.

"No. I employed you because you kiss envelopes before you mail them, and because you surprised me." He paused and closed his eyes. "I like people who surprise me."

Sophie frowned at his profile, aware that she knew practically nothing about this enigmatic man. With his eyes hidden and his head tipped back, he looked thoroughly relaxed, at one with his surroundings. But then again, that wasn't all that surprising if her hunch about him was right.

"Why Norway, Lucien?" Her fingertips trailed over the defined curve of his shoulder as she sipped her champagne.

"Why not here? I like the privacy." The imperceptible tightening of his jaw belied the lightness of his tone.

"It *is* gorgeous," Sophie murmured. "But is there more to it than that?"

"What are you asking, Sophie?" Lucien opened his eyes and met her direct gaze.

"Is this place home for you? I mean… did you grow up here?"

Lucien took a long drink from his champagne flute then placed it down with deliberate care.

"I left Norway on my eighteenth birthday. London is my home now."

Sophie wished he'd look at her, but his eyes were trained on the scrolling skies. She'd already sensed that this place, this country - both were integral to the man he was, but she couldn't work out his feelings for it. He had this beautiful home here, so surely he had to be fond of it, yet there was a toughness to his stance and a steel to the set of his jaw that suggested otherwise.

"Do you miss it when you're in the UK?" Sophie assumed he must. It was way too beautiful not to.

Lucien reached for the champagne bottle. "I didn't, not for a long time."

"So what changed?"

"I did, I suppose." He shrugged non-committally. "I grew up."

"So I guess you must have family here? Parents, brothers and sisters…will you visit them while you're here?" She trailed off uncertainly, aware that she was pushing him for information he wasn't necessarily willing to share.

"No. This visit was only ever about fucking you."

Sophie shook her head and laughed lightly, despite the fact that he was blatantly trying to throw the conversation off course.

"We could have done that back home."

"Yes, but here you can't escape me."

"Who said I'd want to?"

"I do. You're still that good girl deep down, Sophie. Home would have pulled you back to it every moment. Here you're free to be the person you want to be, the amazing woman you can be."

Sophie nodded slowly. His reasoning was sound. Being here had severed her attachments to home - at least for the present - and absence had not made her heart grow fonder.

"It's all still there waiting for me though." She sighed heavily. "What am I going to do about everything, Lucien?"

"What do you want to do?"

Sophie exhaled slowly and shook her head, her mind far away in the UK.

"I don't know. I have to talk to Dan I guess, about his affair, and now about my affair."

Lucien's mouth twisted to one side. "Don't make the mistake of thinking you are the same as he is, Sophie. If he'd been a real husband, you wouldn't be here now."

"How can you know that?"

"Because you're soft, and kind, and good. All the things he isn't."

Sophie registered each compliment, but she didn't feel any of those things. She was an adulterous cheat, every bit as much as Dan.

"You don't know him, Lucien… he's not a bad person."

Lucien shrugged. "I don't need to know him to understand him."

Sophie reached for her glass and swallowed a big gulp of champagne, but the sparkling wine and dazzling views couldn't calm the swirl of emotions inside her.

Lucien looked at Sophie's profile, at the dejected set of her mouth, and that same dull, haunted expression in her eyes that he'd seen the first time he'd met her.

Just talking about her husband had been enough to instantly paint shadows on her face.

What was seeing him again going to do?

What was hearing his confession of an affair spanning more than two years going to do?

The only thing he wanted to do right at that moment was put the sparkle back in her eyes.

He reached out and topped up her glass, then slipped under the bubbling water and resurfaced on his knees face to face with her.

"I think it's time I removed that acorn for you."

Unshed tears still glittered on her eyelashes, but a trembling laugh bubbled from her throat at the broken tension. He could see her turmoil, and he could feel her fear, and he just wanted to make her stronger, tougher and ready to fight. If it was up to him, he'd have had her husband taken care of, one way or another, and be done with it – and he could have made it happen - but he knew that that wasn't the type of resolution Sophie wanted.

Her nipples bobbed rosy and pert in front of him, and he dipped his head to take one into his mouth. *Christ, she was sexy.* He rolled his tongue around the pink nub, enjoying her gratified moan when he closed his lips over it and sucked. His cock stiffened as her nipple turned to rock in his mouth, taut and straining for more attention from his flickering tongue.

When he glanced up, he found her eyes closed, damp tears on her cheeks and her lower lip snagged behind her teeth. She looked trapped somewhere between rapture and despair, and he needed to tip the scales in the right direction.

He moved up her body and covered her mouth with his own, a slow kiss designed to chase the lingering demons from her mind. From the way her tongue responded to his and her hands crept into his hair, he knew he'd succeeded. She arched into him now, her breasts against his chest, his cock between her legs.

It was all about her. About making her feel wanted, about making her eyes shine with satisfaction instead of tears.

When she rocked her hips forwards and invited him inside, Lucien accepted without thought or question. He cradled her body in his arms and thrust slowly, feeling her tightness enfold every inch of him.

She closed her eyes, and he kissed them.

Sophie's body flowed around him like silk, and it didn't feel like fucking. It felt like connecting, and soothing, and like other feelings that he didn't care to give a name to. He slipped his arms around her body under the water as he sensed the beginnings of her orgasm, and as she came he stood and thrust hard, his deft fingers massaging the acorn inside her.

Lucien lost control as Sophie's hips ground hard against his, as the frantic, erotic pulse of her orgasm around his cock had him coming with her. Water cascaded from their hot bodies as they stilled, and Lucien gently eased the acorn out of her splayed bottom. Sophie buried her face in his neck, exhausted, and for a few seconds, Lucien just held her warmth close against his and watched the light show overhead.

He wasn't a man given to romance, but the perfect weight of this woman in his arms and the majesty of the skies above them filled him with an unexpected sense of peace.

Moments later he carried her through the quiet rooms of his home with her head on his shoulder, and by the time he lowered her down onto the bed, she was asleep, tear tracks still just visible on her cooling pink cheeks. When he brushed a blonde strand of hair out of her eyes she sighed and turned her face into his palm, looking for comfort in his touch even as she slept.

Long buried emotions forced their way to the surface as he curled around her and spooned her body into his.

Comfort, sweeter than he'd ever found from a woman's touch.

Fear, spikier than he'd felt for anyone since the day his mother had died.

Anger, sharper than he'd sensed it since the last time he'd laid eyes on his father.

Bile rose in his throat at the thought of the man whose actions had driven his mother to her death.

How dare Sophie's husband push her to this?

How could he put her at risk for the sake of a cheap thrill?

As Sophie's husband and Lucien's father meshed together in his mind, he tightened his hold around her pliant, sleeping form. The quilt settled soft and warm over their shoulders, and he fought to match his heartbeat to her slow, steady breathing pattern.

There was only one thought in his mind as sleep claimed him.

He would protect this woman.

He wouldn't fail again.

Chapter Twenty-Six

Sophie opened her eyes in the half-light of early morning, disorientated by the unfamiliar bed linen and the unfamiliar man sleeping beside her. With one arm flung over his head and the other splayed out to the side, Lucien was utterly peaceful, quite the opposite of his wakeful state. She watched him for a while, trying not to let guilt and dread impinge on the tranquillity of the silent Norwegian dawn. It was something she was never likely to see again. After today, she'd never wake up next to Lucien Knight again.

Real life seemed a world away, but within twenty-four hours she'd be back in her own little house with her own big problems. She closed her eyes for a minute and breathed deeply, then opened them again slowly.

She was ready. Now fully awake and resolved to make the very best of the day, she slid out of bed and into the white towelling robe that hung on a hook on the back of the door, then headed downstairs in search of coffee.

Twenty minutes later, Lucien found her sitting on the deck with a fur blanket around her shoulders and a steaming mug of coffee cradled in her hands.

"You're up early." His breath crystallised in the cold morning air.

Sophie nodded and reached for the cafetière and extra mug she'd prepared for him. He looked lethally gorgeous in black lounge pants and nothing else, the tight buds of his nipples the only indication that he felt the chill on his sculpted body.

"Coffee?"

"Swim?" He inclined his head towards the still, glittering waters of the fjord.

"Are you kidding? It's freezing out here."

In answer, he dropped his lounge pants and stood naked on the deck.

"Do I look like I'm kidding?"

Sophie stared at him, dry mouthed with surprise and lust at the sight of him naked. His cock sprang to attention despite the temperature. She was fast learning that it always did.

She ran her tongue over her lips, and Lucien's appreciative eyes flickered, assessing her reaction.

"Hold that thought, Ms. Black."

He turned and strode out on the small jetty that butted into the water from the decking, giving Sophie the chance to admire his taut rear and the wolf lounging across his shoulder blades. Without hesitation or a backward glance, he executed a perfect dive and sliced into the icy waters of the fjord.

Sophie breathed in sharply as he surfaced and shook the water from his hair, droplets shimmering all around him in the pale morning sunlight.

Jesus, he was magnificent. She watched the water sluice over his muscles as he carved through it with long purposeful strokes that barely rippled the surface. When he climbed back onto the deck a few minutes later and strode towards her, Sophie was quivering in anticipation. She set her cup down, for fear of giving herself away with spilled coffee. Watching Lucien emerge from the lake deserved one hundred percent of her attention. *Move over Mr. Darcy, there's a new man in town.*

"Coffee?" she croaked, repeating her earlier question, now unable to look away from his fast approaching washboard midriff.

In answer, he pushed the fur blanket away from her body, lifted her clean out of the chair, and threw her over his shoulder.

The shock of his unexpected move made her yelp and bang her fists on his back. *No! Was he going to throw her in the water?*

"Lucien, put me down! I can't swim!" She wriggled ineffectively, and he paused to lift her robe and lightly smack her naked, exposed bottom.

"Behave. You're not going in the fjord."

Sophie stilled. "Where are we going then?"

Lucien's fingers caressed where they had stung her a moment before.

"Back to bed. I want you for breakfast."

After a second, more nutritionally though less sexually satisfying breakfast of scrambled eggs and smoked salmon, Lucien suggested that Sophie might like to go and choose some walking boots from the boot room by the entrance door.

She looked up, surprised.

"Are we going out?"

"You seemed captivated by the view outside earlier. I thought you might like to see it close up."

He was right; she'd been thoroughly entranced by the view, especially when it involved a soaking wet, naked Viking. She wasn't much given to hiking, but for him, she'd give it a go.

Lucien glanced at his watch and pushed his chair back.

"I have a couple of business calls to attend to first, though – I'm afraid they can't wait." He picked up his coffee cup and pushed back his seat. As he passed her chair he leaned down and kissed her full on the lips, unhurried and laden with desire. "Dress warm, Princess," he murmured, and her heart softened at his solicitude.

"But don't wear any knickers."

"I can't believe how beautiful it is out here." Sophie turned her head and shaded her eyes to watch a bird of prey swoop down to catch something it had spotted in the undergrowth. They'd been walking for a little over half an hour, and already they seemed to be in a wilderness created just for them. Vibrant, autumnal russet reds and mustard golds covered the ground of the forest they walked alongside, and across the fjord the towering, grey-granite faces of the Alps donned jaunty white snow caps against the pale blue sky.

Back home in England, Sophie was accustomed to being hemmed in by the dense buildings and the bustle and traffic of city life, but out here she found she could really breathe. It was vast, and clean, and gloriously devoid of anyone but them. She snuggled her face into the soft, striped scarf she'd found in Lucien's boot room, glad of its warmth against the chill in the air. Even under the wide, blue skies and pale, watery sunshine, there was no denying that the Arctic air held more than enough bite to turn cheeks pink and unprotected fingers cold.

She'd dressed carefully, hyper-aware of Lucien's parting words as he'd left her after breakfast. She'd deliberated over whether to defy him and wear knickers, stepping in and out of them at least twice before making her final decision.

She'd settled on comfortable jeans with her favourite supersoft, slouchy, black sweater, then added a well-padded red ski jacket and winter woollies from Lucien's boot room. She'd left her hair loose and gone for minimal makeup - the barest flick of mascara and lip-gloss. This environment screamed out for naturalness, and Sophie willingly complied.

Lucien was similarly attired for the elements: he even managed to make winter-wear sexy. His faded jeans clung to his lean muscles and his black windproof jacket worked to highlight his golden skin and steel eyes.

He turned to look at her. "It's this way." He reached for her hand and led her into the forest, leaves and twigs crackling beneath the weight of their boots.

"Are we headed somewhere particular?" she asked, as they moved deeper into the canopy of the trees.

Lucien's mouth crinkled at the edges. "Yes."

"Is it a secret?"

"No."

Sophie rolled her eyes. They appeared to be playing the yes and no game.

"Is this non-secret place much further?"

In answer, Lucien put his hand on the small of her back and propelled her forward. Sophie found herself emerging from the cover of the trees into a circular clearing. Sunshine slanted down onto the glass-like surface of the pool at its centre, but it was the spectacular waterfall that stole Sophie's breath away. Crystal clear, it streamed down the craggy rock face that towered along the side of the clearing, its splash a musical backing track in the otherwise silent afternoon.

It was the mystical cascade from all the fairy stories she'd loved as a child; a magical, secret glade.

"If Hansel and Gretel came out of the woods right now, I wouldn't be surprised," she murmured, enchanted. Not that there was anything childish about the man beside her, nor about the sensations happening between Sophie's legs, thanks to the friction of jeans worn without knickers.

"Nobody here but us, Princess."

Sophie accepted Lucien's outstretched hand as he led her to the water's edge, so clear that she could see the stones on the bottom of the pool and the tiny fish darting close to the surface. She reached down and trailed her fingers in the ice-cold water.

"You're not planning on skinny dipping again, are you?" she asked. "Because gorgeous as this is, there's no way you're getting me in there."

"Relax. No swimming required."

They walked around the clearing and came to a halt near the waterfall. Sophie watched it, mesmerised, but when she turned her face up to speak to Lucien, the expression on his face stole the words from her lips.

He was somewhere far away from her, and wherever his memories had taken him, it wasn't a happy place.

She reached a tentative hand up to touch his cool cheek and

found him as graven as the rock face behind him.

"You look miles away."

His eyes were clouded with emotion when he refocused and looked down at her.

"No, I was right here, just on a different day."

"This is a regular haunt of yours, then? Don't tell me… this is where you bring all the girls?" Sophie wanted to blow away the shadows from his eyes, hoping he'd smile at her teasing.

"I haven't been up here in almost twenty years."

"A childhood hide-out, then?"

She saw the shutters roll down on his emotions, and a predatory light replaced the dullness in his eyes.

"Too many questions, Ms. Black."

He backed her against the nearest tree and lowered his head, his kiss hot and heavy on her lips. His tongue plunged into her mouth and flipped the kiss from sensual to sexual, and his clever fingers unwound the scarf from her neck, freeing more skin for him to stroke and kiss.

Swept up in his sudden switch from contemplative to sexy, Sophie didn't register anything unusual about the way he linked her hands together behind the tree trunk. It was only when she felt the knotted scarf tighten around her wrists that she realised what was happening.

He'd tied her to the tree. An instinctive tug revealed that she was well and truly bound.

Chapter Twenty-Seven

"Would now be a good time to tell you I used to be a boy scout?" Lucien asked.

Somehow, the idea didn't ring true.

"Why have you tied me to a tree?" she demanded. He plucked the woollen hat from her head and unzipped her jacket.

"It's a game."

"A game?"

He nodded. "You'll like it." He lifted her hair so it fell behind her shoulders and kissed her exposed neck. "It's called *Let's show Sophie how fucking beautiful she is.*"

Sophie's breath caught in her throat. "Lucien…"

He lifted her sweater and fresh, cold air hit her midriff, then he bent and kissed her navel and all she registered was heat.

He straightened and kissed her parted lips again, leaving her breathless.

"Your husband is cheating on you."

Sophie frowned, blindsided by Lucien's strange combination of serious conversational matter with sexual stimulation.

He moved her sweater higher to reveal her bra. His gaze scorched her skin even as the air cooled it. He reached out and covered her breasts with his hands.

"Shall I have him killed?" He pinched her nipples, already stiffened by cold air and desire. Sophie squirmed, but the soft scarf held fast.

"No!" She hoped he was joking. *Was he?* "Lucien, do we have to have this conversation while I'm tied to a tree?"

"Yes." He pulled down the nude-coloured lace cups of her bra and exposed her nipples. "The stupid bastard doesn't appreciate the fact that you have perfect tits."

He lowered his head and sucked on first one nipple then the other. His hot mouth fastened hard over her, and the cold breeze on her lick-dampened flesh served only to heighten the incredible sensation.

When he popped the top button of her jeans, she gasped. "Lucien, don't. What if someone walks by?"

He looked up at her from between her breasts.

"They probably won't."

"Probably isn't good enough. Please … can't we just …" The flustered words died on her lips when he stood and pressed his body firmly against hers and the cold material of his jacket crinkled against her skin.

"If anyone came by, which they won't, they'd be fucking lucky to see you like this. Yet another thing your husband seems to take for granted."

Even his fingers on the waistband of her jeans couldn't take the sting out of his words about Dan, mostly because she knew he was right.

"It's complicated, Lucien."

"Why so?" His thumbs drew circles on her hipbones.

"Because…" she struggled to hang onto her train of thought. "You wouldn't understand. He's just not like you."

She felt him exhale scornfully. "You mean he's dull, short and wears fuck-awful suits?"

Inappropriate laughter bubbled in her throat. "No, he's none of those things. He's …"

Lucien's fingers unpopped the last of her buttons, and the brush of his fingertips against her pubic bone rendered her speechless.

"He's what, Sophie?" he whispered against her throat.

She shrugged, pained, and excited. "I don't know… he's bored… with me… I guess?"

Lucien swore under his breath and dragged her jeans down her hips.

"Don't justify his fucking appalling behaviour by blaming yourself."

Sophie looked down at him, shocked by the roughness in his voice and his hands, and ridiculously turned on by the lewd feeling of her jeans around her knees and the cold breeze between her legs. He leaned against her as he stood and cupped her bottom in his big, warm hands.

"Why do you think he fucks someone else when he should be fucking you?"

Sophie dragged cold air into her lungs, unable to breathe properly. Lucien's words lay like acid on her heart, yet his fingers soothed away the pain of the burn.

"I guess I'm just not enough for him anymore," she whispered. It was the fear she'd kept hidden even from herself.

Lucien's game was turning out to be one with high emotional stakes, and she was pretty sure it was a game she couldn't win. She jolted as his fingers bit into the flesh of her bottom.

"Bullshit. Where's your backbone?" He slid his arm between their bodies and touched between her legs. When his mouth covered hers, his breathing was as laboured as her own.

"I'll tell you why he does it, Sophie," Lucien whispered as his deft fingers found her clitoris. "He does it because he can. It's no more complicated than that."

His words were in her ears and her head, yet her mind was unable to process them over the sensations of his hand between her legs.

"Monogamy isn't natural. Not for men, anyway." He pushed two fingers deep inside her and her knees buckled. "For women, maybe, but not for men."

He dragged his open mouth up the curve of her neck as his fingers worked between them. Sophie found she wasn't bothered any more about the possibility of strangers discovering them in the clearing, because she so much wanted the orgasm Lucien was pushing her towards. Yet something in his words stopped her from giving herself over to it. He was wrong. After the week she'd just spent with him, she knew very well that women were every bit as capable of cheating as men.

"I never thought I'd cheat, yet here I am, tied to a tree by a... a... Norwegian sex mogul." *Jeez. Where had that come from?*

"Sex mogul?" he muttered incredulously. He shot her a look, then shrugged. "I've been called worse."

He dropped to his knees and pushed his face into her sex, making Sophie moan as he flicked his tongue over her clitoris. She wanted to open her thighs wider but her jeans held her in constraint. Something about the awkwardness served only to increase the sexiness of the act, and it certainly didn't impede Lucien's skill or concentration. He parted her lips with his fingers and buried his tongue inside her folds, sucking and fingering her swollen clitoris until her body started to shake with pleasure.

He unzipped his coat and slid up the length of her body, unbuttoning his jeans as he did so. "Sex mogul," he repeated under his breath. "A sex mogul who's about to fuck you." He had his jeans down and a condom on in a matter of seconds, then positioned himself against her and thrust hard. Sophie cried out at the swift intimacy of the act, at the searing fullness of him, at the relentless friction of his cock sliding against her clitoris. It wasn't gentle. It was pure, hard fucking, and she orgasmed with a scream almost as soon as he was inside her.

Lucien's eyes blazed bright with hot lust, and Sophie found herself desperate to hold his face in her hands, to soothe away the tension from his jaw.

He pulled back. "Does it feel this good when he screws you?" His voice came out as a harsh rasp as he slammed into her, making her gasp. Sophie shook her head, unable to say out loud that no, no one in her life had ever made her feel like this. His mouth was all over hers, clashing teeth, sliding tongues, and his fingers curled possessively around her hips to hold her steady as he pumped.

"Does it?" he ground out, his eyes boring into hers. "Answer me, Sophie. Say. The. Fucking. Words."

She closed her eyes as he tipped his hips and almost lifted her feet from the forest floor, his cock deeper inside her than she'd ever experienced. Tears constricted her throat and made it difficult to speak. "No," she whispered.

"I can't hear you."

"No. No. No!" The words wrenched from her throat, a raw, emotion-filled admission to herself and to Lucien that no, Dan never made her feel this way. That no man had ever made her feel so soaked in lust, or so filled with dark desire, or so powerful and revered and beautiful.

Lucien's animal, triumphant moan filled her ears, and in answer, a second, even more intense orgasm tightened her body. Slam. Slam. Slam. He clutched her as he came, and she bucked against the base of his shaft as her own release overcame her again in a glittering explosion of pleasure.

Instantly gentle now, Lucien loosed the scarf from her hands and folded her against his chest. She wrapped her arms tightly around him inside his coat and buried her face in his neck, unsure whether he was holding her, or she was holding him.

In the woods, their sex had turned primal. It had certainly brought out the beast in Lucien, brutally dragging the admissions about Dan out of her. But now it was over, Sophie found she was glad of it. He'd freed her from the fear that she'd driven Dan into the arms of another, that she just wasn't woman enough to hold him. Lucien had made her realise that she couldn't fix her marriage on her own, because she wasn't the one who'd broken it in the first place.

More than that, he'd let her see how much power she had within herself: that she, Sophie Black, was enough to drive a man wild. If Dan didn't see that, then he didn't deserve her love.

She instinctively tightened her arms around Lucien, holding him in wonder for giving her the most intensely erotic sex she'd ever known, and in gratitude for giving her the confidence to step back into her old life again as a woman to be reckoned with.

She didn't pretend to understand what made Lucien tick. He might run a string of sex clubs and adult stores, but in his own way he was turning out to be just about the most moral man she'd ever met.

Chapter Twenty-Eight

Back on the threshold of the lodge, Lucien was hailed by his groundsman. It was clear from his expression that he was keen to have a detailed discussion with his boss. Sophie waved Lucien away when he threw her an apologetic glance, happy to make her own way to the kitchen in search of coffee.

And that is where she'd fully intended to go, at first walking straight on past the open door of Lucien's study. But then she hesitated. It had been closed when he'd given her the guided tour and she hadn't given it a thought, but now it stood open and there was a chance to peep behind the curtain. Lucien gave away so little of himself, yet he seemed to know so much of her. Maybe gathering a little more information, understanding a little more, would help her to see behind the façade he'd chosen to reveal.

She glanced uncertainly up and down the deserted corridor, acutely aware that an open door was not necessarily an invitation to enter. Then her curiosity overcame her scruples and she stepped inside.

The room was similarly furnished to the rest of the lodge, yet subtly different. More spartan, more pared down, distilled to reflect the essence of the man who used it.

A large, sleek desk dominated the space, and Sophie slid into the oxblood leather swivel chair behind it to survey the room. Floor-to-ceiling windows created a glass wall looking out over the fjord, more expressive than any mural or expensive artwork could ever have been. Sophie was fast learning that this building was all about making the most of that beautiful vista: every room paid homage to the slice of alpine heaven beyond.

Her eyes moved back into the confines of the study, hungry for knowledge, now that she'd allowed herself to trespass into Lucien's sanctuary. It was bereft of ornament or art, which served only to highlight the one personal possession in the room.

Sophie reached out and touched a finger against the silver frame of the large black and white photograph on Lucien's desk, recognising straight away the unmistakable features of the blonde child with the shining eyes. He couldn't have been more that ten in the picture, but even as a young boy, Lucien had been breathtaking. His defined cheekbones were softened by the bloom of youth, and laughter lit up the smile that cracked his face wide open.

But it was the innocent look of love in his eyes that made Sophie's heart contract with emotion. Lucien's laughter and adoration were all directed towards the woman alongside him in the shot, her arms wound around his slender shoulders. She was elegantly dressed in black, with her blonde hair drawn away from her face. Discreet diamonds glinted in the delicate bracelet around her wrist.

Her gaze was focused on Lucien as she looked down, and even without the benefit of her full features turned towards the camera it was obvious that the woman could only be Lucien's mother. The connection between them jumped out from behind the glass, and the private joke they shared excluded the world around them. Sophie sighed at the tenderness of the picture, the unbreakable bond of love between a devoted mother and son.

Holding the frame in her hands, Sophie studied the relaxed set of the boy Lucien's shoulders and the carefree expression on his face. The man she'd come to know over the last few days was all hard angles and taut muscles, but more than that, he was all about being in control of himself and in charge of those around him. He radiated a low frequency of danger at all times, and Sophie sensed that if he needed to be, he would be utterly ruthless. What had happened to him? Where had his softness gone, the openness she saw in the picture?

Sure, everyone grows up, but the child in the photograph was a world away from the man whose arms she'd just left.

"What are you doing in here?"

Sophie's head jerked up guiltily at the sound of Lucien's carefully controlled voice from the doorway. She'd been so engrossed in her thoughts that she hadn't heard his approaching footsteps, or realised that he was at the door watching her.

"I just… I wanted to…" She was thoroughly flustered, and well aware that the more she stumbled over her words, the more guilty she made herself sound.

"You wanted to what, Sophie?"

She hadn't heard that tone in his voice before. Dead flat, and all the more predatory for its quietness.

Sophie glanced down at the frame still in her hands, and carefully set it back on the desk. So she was in his office. It wasn't the crime of the century, he hadn't expressly asked her not to come in here, and she hadn't snooped around. Not really. The photograph was easily the most arresting thing in the office: the austerity of the room seemed designed to draw the eye to it, so looking at it had been a natural response. She settled her shoulders back and met his eyes.

"The door was open. I didn't realise it was off limits."

Lucien's unreadable gaze slid to the photograph frame, and then slowly back to Sophie.

"It's a beautiful shot," she said softly, watching him for a reaction. Practised as he obviously was at hiding his emotions, Lucien couldn't stop the pulse that flickered along his tense jaw, nor the way his throat moved as he swallowed hard. Several seconds passed before he spoke again.

"Yes." He paced across the room to the windows, his face in profile as he watched the fjord beyond. "I'd prefer it if you didn't come in here again."

It was a clear and direct dismissal, and it frustrated the hell out of Sophie. He'd employed the same tactic last night in the jacuzzi, slamming the brakes on in the face of any questions that went beyond the here and now.

"Is it your mother?"

She saw his throat move again, but his eyes remained fixed on the view.

"It is."

"She's stunning."

Lucien nodded slowly. "She was."

Sophie drew in a breath. "I'm sorry."

"What for?"

"You obviously…" Sophie glanced back at the picture with new comprehension, then up at Lucien's deceptively passive profile. "You must miss her."

"Must I?"

Sophie frowned, aware that he was deliberately making the conversation as difficult as possible.

He turned to her. "Look, I need to make a couple of calls, Sophie. Would you mind…?" His eyes strayed to the door.

"Why do you do that?" Sophie asked, making no move to rise from his chair.

Lucien audibly sighed. "Do what?"

"Change the subject whenever I ask about personal stuff."

He shrugged and rolled his eyes, a deliberate display of nonchalance that didn't fool Sophie for a second.

"I don't. There's just nothing to say."

"But surely you have family here in Norway?"

His jaw set hard again and his nostrils flared slightly. Sophie knew she was pushing him, but she wasn't ready to stop. The scales of knowledge were currently tipped too far in his favour and she wanted to redress the balance.

He shrugged. "Some."

"Brothers… sisters?"

"Why does this matter?"

"Because it does, Lucien. You're happy enough to delve into

179

my marriage. Surely I can ask questions, too?"

His eyes darkened as he considered his response. "Fine." He crossed his arms over his chest, a defensive wall. "No brothers. No sisters. My mother is dead. Anything else?"

Sophie baulked at the blunt delivery of his words, and the bleakness that lay behind them.

"I'm sorry," she murmured again.

"Don't be. It was a long time ago and I'm a big boy. I can look after myself."

She didn't doubt it. But still something held her in the chair, even though he'd made it clear he wanted her out of his office and for this conversation to be over.

"And your father?"

Lucien's eyes narrowed, and Sophie noticed the way his fingers bit into his upper arms.

"Enough, Sophie."

So that was it. "Is he here in Norway?"

Lucien placed his palms down on the desk and fixed her with a fierce, unwavering stare. "I said that's enough."

Sophie drew herself up to a standing position and met his gaze squarely across the expanse of the desk. His breathing was infinitesimally too fast, and his eyes glittered with suppressed anger, although his tone remained even.

"We can talk about it, if it would help," Sophie said softly, sensing that they were dancing around something at the very core of Lucien's psyche.

He laughed harshly. "And suddenly she's a psychiatrist. It's a big leap from a PA, Princess."

Sophie flinched inwardly, hating his sarcastic use of the endearment that up to now had seemed so intimate. "I was just trying to he…"

"I don't need your fucking help." Lucien's words clipped across hers and shocked her into momentary silence. They faced each other across the desk.

"Yet you think I need yours," she said.

"That's different and you fucking well know it."

"Is it?" She leaned towards him. "Why? Because you say so?"

"Yes, damn it." Lucien thumped the desk for emphasis. "And because you needed my help, and I don't need yours, or anyone else's."

His eyes burned into hers, and his tightly balled fists told her that he was every bit as tense as she was.

"He's dead, Sophie, okay? All of this was too long ago to matter, and it's no one's business but mine, but just for the record, my father is dead. Happy now?"

Stricken, Sophie searched Lucien's face for traces of any expression but anger, but it was all there was. She didn't understand what lay behind it, but something had happened to this man. Somewhere along the line, something big and ugly had happened to burden him with this heavy chip of utter self-containment he carried around on his shoulders.

She glanced down at the photograph one last time, then up again at the man the laughing child had become.

"No. I'm a long way from happy, Lucien," she murmured. "I'll leave you to your calls." She turned to walk out of the room.

He was behind her before she made it to the door. He crushed her body against the wall with his own, his hands pushed into her hair. "I'm sorry, Princess. I'm sorry."

Sophie closed her tear-filled eyes and held him, wishing her touch could melt away the iron tension from his shoulders and the bleak sadness from his eyes. She'd leaned on him hard to find out more about him, and all she'd succeeded in doing was unearthing memories that obviously hurt him to talk about.

She gentled his harsh breathing with tender hands and smoothed her fingers over the silk of his hair, until finally he lifted his head and kissed her. His lips moved slow and sweet over hers, balm to soothe the sting of his earlier harsh words.

"I'm sorry too," she whispered into his mouth, opening her jaw to let his tongue slide in. She could feel his heartbeat strong against her own, and his erection hardening against her belly.

Shaky fingers pulled at clothes in search of the comfort and warmth of naked skin, and they dissolved the tension in the only way they knew how, meshed together on Lucien's office floor.

Chapter Twenty-Nine

Lucien refilled Sophie's wine glass after lunch, then pushed his chair back. The meal his housekeeper had prepared for them had been delicious, yet they'd both been subdued after their tempestuous morning.

"I need to go out for a while this afternoon."

Sophie nodded, oddly relieved at the prospect of some time alone. Every moment with Lucien was full throttle, and the experiences of the day so far had left her feeling raw and exposed. Her body ached, and her heart ached even more.

She needed a deep bubble bath to soothe her muscles, and some precious space to think. In less than twenty-four hours she'd be back in London with Dan, and as yet she had no clue what on earth she was going to do. All she knew was that the next few hours felt like a stay of execution.

Lucien rested his forehead against the cold side window of the car and stared at the plain, red brick university hospital building. This wasn't his intended destination this afternoon, yet he'd instinctively turned along the drive anyway rather than pass on by. He had no intention of going inside. His fingers closed around the letter inside his jacket pocket, not caring about the fact that he was screwing it up to a point where reading it again would be nigh on impossible. He knew what it said without looking at it anyway.

Dear old papa was in here once again for alcohol abuse, only this time around there was every chance he wouldn't make it out again. He'd been a dead man walking ever since his wife killed herself; Lucien was only surprised that it had taken him this long. He had no feelings to offer except disgust and hatred, and what use were they to a dying man?

Let the chaplain hear his father's pleas for forgiveness. Let the cold hand of a stranger be his comfort. Lucien had nothing to give him.

He studied the building and wondered which window sheltered his father. How would he look these days? Lucien had cut all ties with him after his mother's death, choosing to stay with relatives who bore his troubled presence like a cross rather than stay with the pitiful father who pleaded daily for his son's understanding.

Yet wherever Lucien laid his hat, the letters stubbornly followed. His father had tracked his progress around the world and stayed in contact every few months, despite the fact that he never received any acknowledgment that his words had reached his son.

Lucien didn't want to read them, and for many years, he hadn't done so. He chucked them, unopened, one on top of the other, into an old box, unsure why he wasn't just hurling them into the fireplace instead.

As the years slipped by and the letters continued to arrive, Lucien's protective shell hardened enough for him to be able to open them without being engulfed by fury. He wasn't that frightened child anymore.

The letters brought him news of his homeland, of family deaths, and of babies being born who shared his bloodline.

Letter by letter, those paper windows onto the minutiae of day-to-day life in the Arctic Circle rekindled his love for Norway, a bone-deep homesickness to lie on his back in the clearing and watch the skies dance once more.

And so he'd rebuilt his relationship with his motherland, made his peace with the beautiful, cold kingdom that held such bittersweet memories. Returning to Tromso as a successful man had calmed the roar of injustice in his heart. He'd come full circle, and after years of running away, it was fitting that Norway offered him the safe harbour and solace missing from his life in London.

Yet still he didn't contact his father.

He couldn't do it. When all was said and done, the man was responsible for his mother's death, and all the talking in the world could never change that.

He flung the balled up letter onto the passenger seat and threw the car into reverse. He put his foot down as he hit the open road, disgusted with himself for even being there in the first place. There was somewhere else he wanted to be.

Sophie lounged in the steaming bubbles and closed her eyes. If she could freeze time, she'd push the button right now. Lucien had transported her into this fairytale of magical skies and sublime sex, but the adventure had to come to an abrupt end tomorrow. Grey skies and marital discord waited impatiently for her, back in London, and the idea of seeing Dan again made her stomach roll with dread.

Her whole world had revolved around him for her entire adult life; he was all she'd known of love. *But did she still love him now?* She turned the question over in her head. Before she'd met Lucien Knight, she'd have answered yes in a heartbeat, but would it have been the truth? Loving Dan was her default setting, but this week with Lucien had forced her to take an honesty pill when it came to her own emotions.

Sophie reached for the dark glass of Shiraz balanced on the ledge beside the bath and drank deeply. The wine warmed her veins and fortified her with Dutch courage to continue her long overdue personal therapy session.

It was curious really, to stand back and look at the bare facts. Sophie had had an idea that Dan had been seeing someone else for more months than she'd care to admit, yet she'd allowed herself to ignore the mounting evidence. It had been alarmingly easy to consider his alternative explanations plausible rather than face the possible truth and all of its associated ugliness.

Was he aware that she knew? Did he take her lack of challenge as tacit acceptance? Hot shame flushed her cheeks warmer than the steamy bath water. How little must he think of her if that was the case?

She knew in her heart why she'd held her silence. It was simple, really.

She'd wanted him to choose her.

Then along came Lucien Knight, and at one look from him, Sophie had stopped waiting. With one touch, the scales had fallen from her eyes.

Lucien had reminded her how it felt to be adored, and how much she'd missed it.

Memories of Dan tumbled through her mind, and she let them in. Memories of the times he'd been the one taking the time to make her feel adored.

At sixteen, laughing as she rode on the crossbar of his bike all the way home from school. At eighteen, his hair too long and his big easy smile that lit her heart. And on her twenty-first birthday, nervous and down on one knee in the damp leaves as they walked through the park.

Tears slipped from beneath her closed eyelids. Tears for Dan, and for their love that once upon a time had felt too big to break.

Lucien shoved his hands in his pockets and pushed his chin down into his jacket. The cemetery was suitably bleak, and there were no flowers to cheer the grey stone that bore his mother's name.

Would she be proud of the man he'd become? Would he have trodden the same path if she'd lived? He didn't have any answers, or anyone to ask. She'd been gone from his life for more years now than she'd been there, and his recollections of her were all wrapped up in childish memories of wiped tears and goodnight kisses, of scraped knees and snowy Christmas mornings.

It hadn't been a conscious decision to wrap his heart up and bury it along with his mother, yet it had somehow happened anyway. He'd stood at this same graveside all those years back, a man-child, barely a teenager, suddenly alone and bereft of love. No one had come close to melting the ice around his heart since then, though many had tried.

He'd grown up beautiful and rebellious, trouble to everyone and desired all the more for it by the girlfriends who'd littered his past.

Lucien reached out a hand and laid it against the cold, hard stone. Her face was indistinct in his mind now; she was more a feeling than an image. Her memory had kept him safe as he'd grown. She was the only person who'd looked at him and understood his heart.

He scrubbed his hands over his face. He'd come here because he needed to talk and there was no one else to listen.

What was he doing with Sophie Black? Why was he trying to save her? What the fuck did he think he was: Knight by name and Knight by nature? And if that was it, why did he feel more and more like she was the one saving him?

Without even trying, Sophie had gotten under his skin in a way that the many polished and predatory women who'd populated his life and his bed before now had never managed. Her softness and her bravery impressed the hell out of him, and finding her in his arms when he woke seemed to still his ever-present need to get up and fight.

He closed his eyes for a second in silent remembrance, and then turned and walked away.

Chapter Thirty

All cried out and resolved to make the most of these last stolen hours, Sophie returned to Lucien's bedroom and noticed the note he'd propped on the bedside table.

"I've fired up the saunarium for you. Try it, I think you'll like it."

Sophie wandered back into the bathroom, the note still in her hand. Saunarium? Was that the same as a sauna? She'd noticed the wooden door in there yesterday, but the tiered, planked room had been cool and dry when she'd peered in.

It wasn't cool in there anymore.

She glanced down at the white fluffy towel wrapped around her body. Her own private spa session was too good an opportunity to pass up. She grabbed a glass of cold water then stepped inside, instantly aware of ambient heat, and thankful that she was able to breathe easily thanks to the clever mix of heat and humidity. So a saunarium was something between a sauna and a steam room, she realised. Trust Lucien to have the best of both worlds.

Sophie breathed in through her nose and out through her mouth, then settled herself into the corner of the lower bench opposite the door. Her whole body felt infused with heat, as if the warmest sunshine was kissing her skin. Low lights glowed in the ceiling, turning the room into a blissful cocoon.

A sigh of pleasure left Sophie's lips as she leaned back and willed herself to relax. Her tearful session in the bath had proved cathartic on many levels. She'd cried out of regret for the loss of trust in her marriage and sadness at her trampled hopes of forever love with Dan. She'd finally taken off her rose tinted glasses and, come tomorrow, she was ready to grab her life by the scruff of the neck and shake it, hard. She had no idea where the jumbled pieces would fall, but she refused to allow herself to be cowed by fear of the unknown.

Hadn't this week shown her that life could be bigger and better than she'd ever imagined it to be? This fantasy interlude with Lucien wasn't real life, but it would be a lie and a disservice to him to deny that every minute had been anything other than breathtaking.

Still, she had no idea how she could continue working for him after this week. He was hands down the most charismatic, fabulous man she'd ever met, the stuff of every woman's daydreams, but life with him in it felt rather like having her foot jammed on the accelerator. He left her breathless and giddy, and he did things to her body that she didn't even know could be done. She barely knew him, yet he seemed to know her inside out.

She'd climbed out of the bath, and like a snake shedding its skin, she'd left the old Sophie behind. The girl gazing back at her in the steamed up mirror was all new and shiny-eyed, and ready to rock her own world.

Sophie breathed in deeply as she relaxed back onto the saunarium bench. She was warm to the bones. Hot, in actual fact. She opened her eyes and glanced down at her towel, then up again at the doorway. She was certain no one would come in here aside from Lucien, and he was still out pursuing his mysterious business ends. Her fingers unworked the towel from beneath her arms, and with a last glance towards the door, she unwrapped it and let it fall open on the bench.

She was naked in Lucien's saunarium.

Feeling suddenly exposed, even though she was alone, Sophie took a long slug of cold water and pushed her damp hair back from her forehead.

Thoughts of Lucien in the woods earlier crept unbidden into her mind when she closed her eyes. Her wrists still tingled from where he'd tied her up, and her body still fizzed with the memory of her orgasms. She glanced down at her body, flushed and glistening damp, and wondered what she'd do if Lucien were to open the door at that very moment.

Would she grab for the towel to cover up, or would she invite him in? *Easy.* Her feeling of ultra-relaxation morphed slowly into nerve-tingling arousal as she imagined him. Yes, she could well imagine Lucien using this room… big, bronzed and butt naked. Her hands smoothed down the length of each of her damp arms, and then settled lightly over her breasts at the thought of him undressed.

She closed her eyes and massaged her own warm flesh, slick with a sheen of moisture from the damp heat. Her nipples peaked beneath her sliding thumbs, the imprint of Lucien's mouth fastening over them in the woods that morning seared clear on her memory. She sighed as she laid her head back against the stepped wooden bench behind her, caught up in the heated recollection of Lucien's hands on her body. That little moan of appreciation he'd made low in his throat when he'd discovered she'd obeyed his command to leave her knickers at home. The way he'd licked her lips as he slid his hand inside her jeans and found himself cupping her bare sex. She cupped it herself now, mirroring his actions to recreate that throb of anticipation between her legs.

Sophie caught her lip between her teeth and gasped softly as she slipped her fingers inside her slick folds, one knee lifted on the bench.

She was so warm, and so open, and completely caught up in her own private re-enactment of the morning's events beside the waterfall. Jesus, he'd tied her up, anyone could have seen. Her fingers sought her clitoris as she recalled Lucien on his knees pushing his tongue into her sex. He'd licked her here… it had felt like this… Sophie arched as she touched herself, her fingers as insistent as Lucien's dexterous tongue had been. She squeezed her eyes tightly shut as the sensations intensified.

"Need a hand, Princess?"

She yelped with surprise as her eyes flew open and her fingers jumped away from her body. She'd been too far down the line to ecstasy to notice the door opening. She ought to be mortified – the old Sophie certainly would have been - but he was naked, and the molten heat in his eyes told her not to be, as did the erect curve of his cock against his hard, smooth abdomen.

Had she conjured him up by the power of thought alone? He stepped inside and dropped to his knees between her legs.

"Carry on."

She looked down into the dangerous gleam of his eyes as he laid his head against her inner thigh. Gold on cream. He was close enough to reach out his tongue and lick her, yet he didn't.

"Tell me what you were thinking of just now."

Sophie took a huge fortifying gulp of water. Just a few days ago she'd have played things differently, but right now she willed herself to match his boldness. She tipped a little of the cool water onto her fevered skin and they both watched the rivulets run down between her breasts.

"I was remembering." She let her hand fall casually back between her legs.

He dropped a languorous kiss onto her thigh. "Hmm. Tell me more."

"I was thinking about this morning... in the woods..." She watched him run his tongue over his lips as she opened herself with her fingers. She could feel his breath on her clitoris.

"Which part?"

She reached out a fingertip and traced the full, damp curve of his lower lip, then touched herself. "The part where you put your hand inside my jeans to check if I was wearing knickers."

He lifted an approving eyebrow. "I liked that part too." He kissed the back of her fingers. "What else?"

Sophie could barely get her breath. She was hot, and wet, and desperate for him. She kept her voice steady, with an effort.

"I was thinking about how your tongue felt on me." She circled her clitoris with her fingers as she spoke. "I was imagining you licking me. Right here."

"Here?" He followed the movement of her fingers with the faintest trace of his tongue, making her shudder with pleasure.

"I love the taste of you," he murmured. "Keep talking."

That wasn't so easy with his mouth a whisper away from her sex. "I was thinking about your hard, beautiful cock inside me." He groaned, his heated mouth so close to her, letting her know how much her words were turning him on. It was a heady feeling. "About you fucking me hard against that tree."

His control snapped, and he replaced her hands with his own between her legs, his fingers splayed on her thighs to hold her open. His thumbs slid inside her as he lowered his head to make slow, hypnotic love to her with his mouth, shockingly intimate and mind-numbingly erotic. She wanted it to last a lifetime, but he had her in seconds. Breathless with exquisite pleasure, she watched and felt him worship her. His eyes flickered up and connected with hers as he held her in his mouth while she came. Dangerously dark and glittering, their grey-blue depths were heavy with the promise of a long night ahead.

Chapter Thirty-One

They dressed for dinner.

Lucien looked like James Bond's sexier brother, lethal and dripping with sex appeal. Sophie felt as if she'd stepped onto a film set and been unwittingly cast as his lucky love interest. But of course, as in all the best Bond movies, she was only Lucien's leading lady until the adventure ended.

The food was divine, yet they barely tasted it.

Her knee touched his as she reached for her wine.

His fingers brushed hers as he refilled her glass.

His gaze lingered on her lips as she tested the golden cloudberry puree drizzled around the perfectly set pannacotta.

"This is delicious." She savoured the chilled, velvet cream in her mouth.

Lucien inclined his head as he sampled his own dessert. "It's missing something." He pushed his chair back and headed around the table with his dessert plate in his hand. "What do you think?" He spooned a little of his pannacotta into her mouth, his eyes on her lips. He was in full-on predator mode, and a thrill of anticipation rippled down Sophie's spine.

He rested against the table, and she placed a deliberately casual hand on his leg as she swallowed her mouthful of the faultless dessert.

"Mmm. I see what you mean…"

Lucien's eyes dropped to watch her hand slide up his thigh. In seconds, he pulled her onto her feet against his body.

"You know, I think it needs to be sweeter," he said, and slid down the zipper on her dress.

It pooled on the floor, leaving Sophie outrageously turned on and wearing only her knickers and black suede high heels. His eyes roved over her body, and his tongue touched his lip in concentration as he switched her around to perch on the table. Lucien's fingers were already working open the buttons of his shirt, and he threw it aside a moment later and shifted her to sit more securely on the edge of the table.

It was cold and smooth beneath her bottom, even more so when Lucien dispensed with her knickers a second or two later. He moved in close between her legs, his mouth over hers.

"You should tell the cook to add a little more sugar," she said, massaging his erection through his trousers.

"Hm." Lucien dipped his finger into his dessert and wiped it across Sophie's lower lip. She snaked out the tip of her tongue to taste it, and met his tongue there already doing the same thing. His arms were braced either side of her body as she tilted her head back to let him do a thorough job on her mouth.

"That tastes a little sweeter already," he murmured.

"Not enough, though?" she asked, fully aware that it wouldn't be.

He shook his head, rueful. "Not quite."

Sophie nodded, then dipped her own fingers into the pannacotta and painted her peaked nipples until they resembled the Alps outside the windows. "Would this help, do you think?"

He lifted an approving eyebrow. "Let me check."

He lapped each of her nipples clean, and the connection between his hot tongue and the cold dessert on her flesh made Sophie sigh with pleasure. His cock was as hard as rock under her hand.

"Well?" she whispered, besieged by the rampant lust in his eyes when he straightened.

"It's almost there." He reached behind her, and in one swift move he swept the entire contents of the dining table onto the floor.

Everything besides his pannacotta.

His warm hands spanned her waist and shifted her backwards on the table, and he spread her legs wide. Sophie knew full well where he was headed, and her body trembled with anticipation. She bit her lip as his fingers dipped into his dessert, and her body tightened with erotic shock as he smeared the chilled cream between her legs. He paused momentarily to admire his handiwork; a layer of thick peaked swirls that covered her modesty in the lewdest possible way.

"Taste me." She was halfway to begging, and that cocky half grin touched Lucien's lips.

"Say that again."

"Please, Lucien. Taste me."

Lucien dropped his head, a slow drag of his tongue up the entire length of her sex. Sophie's stomach twisted as she watched the cream transfer from her body to his tongue. "Better?"

His hand splayed on her stomach. "It's fucking delicious."

His thumb massaged the cream into her pubic bone, a whisper away from her clitoris, and when he finally dropped his head and devoured her, the switch from playful to deadly serious had her almost coming on the spot. His tongue and lips were all over her sex. Sucking, lapping, licking her clean.

Sophie dropped back onto the cool tabletop and pressed her hands to her flushed cheeks, closer to orgasm with every stroke of his tongue. He pulled her to the edge of the table and unbuckled his trousers, then thrust his sheathed cock inside her without any need for preamble.

Sophie was hot, wet and ready, and he was gloriously hard, fast and filthy. She came almost as soon as he slammed into her, and Lucien came seconds after. It was too intense to last more than that couple of moments, but they were easily the sexiest moments of Sophie's life.

Lucien threw a log on the fire and settled down alongside Sophie, their backs leaning against the sofa. She was all golden curves and warmth in the amber glow of the flames, one leg folded in front of her, supporting her elbow, the other stretched out so she could wriggle her toes into the sheepskin rug. She'd slipped her knickers back on and half buttoned his shirt over her body after dinner, typical gestures of bashfulness despite the fact that she'd let him screw her senseless on the dining table.

"You okay?" he murmured, twisting a strand of her hair lightly around his finger. She sipped her generous measure of brandy and nodded, eyes fixed on the dancing flames.

"I think so." Her features were melancholy in profile. "Just sad that this is the end."

He wasn't sure if she was referring to their time together or her marriage. Or both. He slipped his hand beneath the weight of her hair to massage the back of her neck.

She tilted her head forward a little to take full advantage of his ministrations, then sighed and rolled her shoulders.

"I just wish I could press the pause button, I'm dreading tomorrow."

"I'd prefer the rewind button," Lucien said, pleased by the gentle smile that tilted her lips as he glanced up at the clock. It was a little after ten. "Anyway, we don't need to leave for a few hours yet, and I'm not planning on sleeping."

She leaned back and turned to face him. "Thank you for bringing me here, Lucien." Her eyes were round and serious, and twin pink apples kissed her creamy cheeks. Everything about her spoke of goodness and wholesomeness, which made the erotic kick of unbuttoning her inhibitions all the more addictive.

She glowed, and he basked in it. "You're welcome any time, Ms. Black."

Shadows dulled the brightness of her eyes. They both knew she wouldn't come back here again after tonight. Their worlds were poles apart, and this had only ever been about one week.

All of that could wait for another day, though. Right now he wanted to banish those shadows, and fast.

"The way I see it, we can spend tonight talking, or we can do something else." He leaned forward and trailed a finger down skin exposed by the deep open V-neck of his shirt. "Personally, I think talking is overrated."

Her eyelids drifted down and her plump lips parted with a soft sigh. His cock stirred in his jeans. Sophie Black's unintentional mix of innocence and sultriness was a lethal combination that had him half way to hard every time he looked at her. It was the main reason he'd given her the job, and the whole reason he'd brought her with him on this trip to Norway.

The latest letter from his father had pulled him back here as surely as if he'd yanked on an invisible string, but having Sophie along for the trip had turned it from an instinctive obligation to a very adult pleasure ride.

He leaned in, and her mouth opened like a flower when he covered it with his own. She tasted of honey laced with brandy. The trace of her tongue over his had his hands moving into her hair to draw her closer, to open her mouth wider, to let him drink more deeply.

A tiny sigh of pleasure escaped her throat as she tipped her head back and let him lead her, and he couldn't resist sliding his hand inside his – now her - shirt to cup the softness of her breast as her tongue slid over his.

Christ, she made his cock ache. Her nipple instantly ripened from velvet soft to a stiff peak when he brushed a slow thumb over it, and he was gratified by the catch in her breathing and the fractional arch of her back. Her body was alive with sensual desire, and he was going to take his sweet time satisfying her tonight.

Sophie felt her breast swell into Lucien's hand as every fibre in her responded to his touch. His unhurried tongue explored her mouth as his other hand smoothed flat over the back of her hair. He was oh so thorough, and all she could think of was right here, and right now. Indistinct music played in the background; late night, laid back sounds that conjured up hazy images of backstreet Parisian bars.

One by one, he opened her shirt buttons, and she shivered with expectation when he eased it off her shoulders. Naked aside from her knickers, she snaked her arms around him and closed her eyes. When he hauled her over to straddle his lap her breasts flattened against his bare chest, finding him firm and warmed from the fire. His hands swept up her spine to twist into her hair, easing her head back to expose her throat to his trail of open-mouthed kisses. She could feel his erection pressed between her legs, separated only by denim and silk. Hard against soft.

Lucien's hands ran down Sophie's spine again to mould her bottom as she conducted her own exploration of his back, committing the smooth planes and taut curves to memory. She couldn't see it, but she knew that the predatory lone wolf slumbered beneath her hands as she stroked his shoulder blades.

He held her breasts in his hands, then lowered his face to them and breathed in deeply.

Sophie arched, greedy for his mouth all over her, his tongue on her nipples, his five o'clock shadow prickling deliciously against the tender undersides of her breasts.

His hair slipped through her fingers, and when he came back up to claim her mouth, his kiss sent her senses reeling.

"Kiss me all night?" She sank her teeth into the fullness of his bottom lip.

"Where?" He tweaked her nipple. "Here?" He ran his finger down her stomach. "Or here?" He traced a barely there line across the top edge of her knickers.

"Or do you want me to kiss you here, Princess?" His fingers scorched against her sex, warm and massaging through the flimsy silk.

Yes, yes, and oh God, yes. She wanted his mouth everywhere. She lifted her hips, and he surprised her by slithering down to lie on his back beneath her, nuzzling between her legs. He was more insistent now, she could feel his tongue probing her through the material.

Oh, he was so, so good.

He moved her knickers aside with his fingers, and Sophie had to hold back the orgasm that hovered ready for him to claim. She wanted it to last, but the slow, insistent stroke of his tongue along her sex was beyond thrilling. Hot… wet… and when he fulfilled her wish and kissed her clitoris, his tenderness overwhelmed her efforts to hold it back any longer. He kissed her through the long blissful tremors, and then slid out from beneath her and hauled her down to sit between his legs. His bent knees bracketed hers as she leaned back against his chest.

"More relaxed now?" She could feel his smile against her ear as he crossed his arms over her body and held her breasts in his hands, the relaxed embrace of comfortable lovers.

"Just a little bit," she laughed shakily, her heart still pounding. Sex with Lucien was a cross between the most sweeping romantic movie and the filthiest porn flick; he was feather gentle and filthy erotic all at the same time.

Sophie had never known such a generous man. He seemed to get off on getting her off, and right at that moment she could feel his still raging erection pressing against the base of her back. She reached a hand behind her and covered his denim-clad crotch. "You don't seem quite as relaxed yourself, though."

"It's what you do to me." He lifted her hair over one shoulder and kissed the nape of her neck. After the week they'd spent together, Sophie knew they weren't just empty words. She slipped her knickers off and scooted around to face him, her hand back on his crotch, her mouth on his. He moaned low and cradled her face in his hands as she unfastened his buttons. He was naked beneath his jeans, as she'd known he would be, and his cock sprang out of its confines, thick, ridged and begging for her attention. Sophie pushed his jeans clear and circled him with her hand between their bodies. He was so ready, she could feel the heavy rise and fall of his chest against her breasts.

"Jesus, Sophie…"

She kissed his closed eyelids, and the sensitive skin beneath his ear as she palmed his length. He was golden and sculpted in the firelight. Beyond beautiful.

"Condom?" she breathed, increasing her speed a little and getting a kick out of the look of almost agonised pleasure on his face. "In my jeans," he muttered, and she reached behind her into his pocket. He ripped it open and sheathed himself, then pulled her back into his lap.

"Sit on me."

Sophie laughed softly into his mouth. "Say that again."

He rocked his hips, rubbing the head of his cock over her clitoris. "Sit on me."

She raised herself up and impaled herself on every glorious inch of him. She sighed with pleasure, holding him as deep inside her body as he could possibly be. Utterly connected, totally lost.

"Fuck... fuck..." Lucien repeated his mantra, his face a study of erotic concentration as Sophie dictated the slow pace of their sex. She mouthed his neck when he tipped his head back, and he licked her nipples when she hollowed her spine.

His hands spanned her waist, and she could feel him holding onto his control as she rocked herself on him. Lust darkened his blue eyes and tensed his jaw, yet he was iron hard and unhurried in his quest to make the moment last for both of them. It was exquisite, and deeply erotic, and Sophie knew it was a memory that would stay with her forever. Her hand on his jaw, she increased the tempo, knowing full well that he wouldn't be able to hold back any longer. His fingers bumped up her spine to curl over her shoulders, holding her down on his jerking hips as he climaxed with a shudder that shook his whole body.

Sophie watched Lucien's face as he came. She saw his teeth clench, and when he opened his blue-grey eyes, she saw raw vulnerability there that was all at odds with the self-assured sex god he usually let the world see.

She laid her hand on his cheek, and he turned and placed a tender kiss against her palm. Then, instinctively, she wrapped her arms around him and drew him against her breast.

Of all the emotions Lucien Knight had aroused in her over the last few days, the one thing she hadn't expected to feel was protective.

Lucien drew in a deep breath as his orgasm ebbed. Somehow, Sophie had turned the tables on him. He'd never felt anything like the orgasm she'd just given him, and over the years he'd had more than his share of beautiful and accomplished lovers.

A butterfly from her chrysalis, she'd emerged even brighter and more spellbinding than he'd imagined. She'd used her body to pleasure him, and in her arms he'd found far more than physical release.

The world had seemed a pretty bleak place standing in the cold graveyard that afternoon, but right now, anchored inside Sophie's naked body with the warmth of the fire on their skin, it seemed pretty damn close to perfect.

Some time just after one and somewhere in between awake and asleep, Sophie moved beneath him again. Tangled limbs. Entwined fingers. Damp cheeks. Bruised hearts.

Chapter Thirty-Two

Sophie settled into her leather recliner on Lucien's jet as it taxied for take off. The velvet black skies of the early hours outside matched the colour of her mood. Her stomach churned with dread, her mind already hundreds of miles ahead in London, playing through possible ways the day might play out.

Where would she be come nightfall?

If only she could rewind the clock and live last night over and over. Lucien had taken her breath away so many times it was a wonder she was still standing. He'd been rampant and rude at the dinner table, and later on he'd been tender because she'd needed him to be. She'd felt like crystal in his hands.

She glanced up as he buckled himself into the seat alongside hers.

"All set?" he asked. Already she could feel the gulf between them widening as reality intruded on their interlude. There was an awkwardness to his tone, and a detached look in his eye.

Or was she imagining those things in him because she felt them herself?

With every passing minute she felt more like the old Sophie, as if she were sliding back into her old, dull skin after a borrowed week covered in burnished gold.

"Ready to go," she murmured. *What other choice did she have? No, I'm not all set? No, turn this plane around, I don't want to go home?*

This had only ever been a one week deal. Now it was over and time to get on with the messy business of real life and cheating husbands and ruptured marriages.

Sophie closed her eyes and swallowed the lump that rose in her throat as the plane took off from Norwegian soil. It was a country she'd never imagined that she would even see, yet within a few short days, she'd fallen completely under its spell. Its sweeping vistas, soaring Alps and mystical skies had imprinted themselves on her forever, as had the big, beautiful Viking at her side now.

Warm fingers covered her own clenched ones, and she opened her eyes.

"I'm all right, really. Just sad to leave."

He nodded. "Today will be okay, Sophie."

"Will it?" She searched his eyes with her own as panic rose in her chest. "I don't think I can face him."

"It's not too late for me to have him taken care of," Lucien said, deadpan, but his eyes were gentle and concerned.

"I just feel so guilty, Lucien."

Lucien shook his head. "Tell me this, then. Would you be here now if he had treated you properly?"

Sophie looked down and studied her wedding ring.

Would she? Could she have resisted Lucien if she'd have been blissfully happy with Dan? She'd have liked to say yes, but she wasn't so sure. It was a big ask. After a week in his company she was under no illusion about the power of his allure.

He reached out and held her shoulders, forcing her eyes up to meet his. "Why should you be the one with moral fibre, when he's the one who has been screwing someone else for months?"

But much as he had a point, this wasn't just about Dan, Sophie thought. It was about her, too. It was about the trail of destruction she was about to wreak on her own life.

"Lucien, I'm going home, and I'm probably about to leave my husband. And I can't work for you any more, not after this. By the end of today I'll most likely be single, possibly homeless, and jobless."

"You aren't going to be jobless. You have a job."

"Don't be ridiculous." She stared at him. How could he think it tenable for her to continue as his PA? "Obviously I can't carry on working for you after this."

"Why not? We haven't lied to each other or made any false promises. We're not kids. We can separate work from play."

Sophie shivered. Wow. He really was as ice-cool as the land they'd just left behind. So analytical, so free of emotional bonds.

"I'm not like you, Lucien. I can't neatly compartmentalise my life into work, and sex." She shrugged. "I'm not a man, I guess."

Something about her words pierced through the ice. She saw it in the narrowing of his eyes and in the sudden stiffness in his jaw.

"Don't throw me in with the likes of your husband, Sophie. Yeah, I like sex, but I'm honest about what I do, and who I do it with. I don't run around behind closed doors getting my kicks from hurting the people I profess to love."

Whoa. Where did that come from?

"Love." She repeated the word distractedly as if she'd never heard it before. It was something she felt she knew very little about these days.

"Yeah, love. That thing that causes nothing but misery and heartbreak, then makes people grow fat on too much ice cream and get ill-advised haircuts when it goes wrong."

Ouch. She was alert again now. What on earth was behind this?

"Have you never been in love, Lucien? Have you never wanted someone so much that your heart roars when you're with them, and every bone in your body aches for them when you're not?"

"No."

"That's it? Just, no?"

"What did you expect?" He shrugged and splayed his hands out to the sides. "Some sorry tale of my poor broken heart? Sorry, Princess."

Sophie shrugged, at a loss. He'd managed to turn his term of endearment into a sneer once again. "I don't know. I don't know. I just…"

"I don't need to label my feelings as love, or shackle some woman to me just for the sake of a big fucking party and a meaningless piece of tat." He glanced down at her wedding ring and she covered it instinctively. It had never left her finger since the day Dan had slid it into place, and however much of a sham it seemed right now, the idea of taking it off felt like removing a piece of herself. Like her whole identity being scraped off with a scalpel.

"Don't say that." She defensively touched the gold band on her third finger.

"Why not? Because the truth hurts?" Lucien's mouth twisted in distaste. "I bet your husband takes his off when he fucks his lover."

Sophie felt his words land like punches. "Do you have to be so blunt?" she shot back at him.

"Yes. Yes I do. Because if I'm not, you'll walk back in there and listen to his platitudes and lies."

"But isn't that *my* choice? Why does it matter to you what I do, Lucien?"

Lucien thumped the arm of his seat in anger and frustration. "Why are you doing this now, Sophie? Why are you doubting all the things you've said and felt this week?"

Sophie sighed heavily. "Because this is my whole life we're talking about Lucien, not an episode of some TV reality show. I have to listen to him, to at least hear his side of the story."

"His side of the story?" Lucien's laugh held no humour. "Is that the part where he falls on his knees and you forgive him?" He gazed at her intently, and Sophie glared right back, noticing the way his throat moved as he swallowed hard. "I'll show you his side of the fucking story."

He reached for his laptop, opened it up, and after a few key-presses, angled the screen towards Sophie, who found herself staring at a series of photographs. She narrowed her eyes, trying to make sense of the images in front of her. But they didn't *make* any sense. Not here, not on Lucien's laptop, not in Lucien's private jet.

Her husband, in an airport with his lover.

Dan laughing in a bar, draped over his lover.

Again on a balcony, his naked lover wrapped around him.

Not wearing his wedding ring.

Sophie couldn't breathe, her lungs were suddenly too tight.

Unable to take her eyes off the screen, her hands flew to her cheeks in shock. After the days she'd just spent with Lucien, she'd forfeited her right to play the victim, yet still her heart shattered into a million pieces at the sight of Dan's arms wrapped around another woman. She wanted to reach inside the screen and touch his smile, to twist his head away from that woman and make him look her way instead.

Those were the arms she'd planned to spend the rest of her life in, and his kiss was the only one she'd ever wanted on her lips.

Tears dampened her cheeks, and a great sob wrenched itself out of her body. Knowing about Dan's affair was one thing. Having images of it forever burned onto her retinas was another. She dropped her face into her hands and cried her heart out.

Lucien closed the screen slowly and placed the laptop back on the table beside him. Watching Sophie cry was excruciating. His every instinct was to reach out and hold her. "Sophie… Princess… I'm so sorry." She flinched when he touched her, and the look in her eyes when she raised her head chilled him to the bone.

"You're sorry? Which bit are you sorry for, exactly, Lucien? The bit where you stalked my husband, or the bit where you used my marital problems to get me into bed? Christ, you must think I'm so stupid." Her words came out in a jumble of tears and shaky breath, but anger held her frame ramrod straight. "You planned this. You knew Dan was cheating, and you saw an opportunity to take something that wasn't yours."

Lucien's mind scrambled to keep up with Sophie's train of thought. She'd got it all very, very wrong.

"Sophie, no." He reached for her hands but she wrenched them away. "That isn't what happened…"

"Really? Because that's *exactly* what it looks like from where I'm sitting. Why, Lucien?" She dragged her hands furiously across her cheeks, smearing mascara tear tracks into zig-zags on her face. "Don't even bother to answer. You're no better than Dan. You're worse in fact, because you're fucking sanctimonious with it." Sophie's lip curled. "Is that your thing? Lucien Knight, honourable Viking seducer, ready to swoop in and rescue damsels in distress? Is that it?" Her fists were balled so tightly that her knuckles gleamed white. "Is it?"

"Yeah. Because I'm a regular Thor." Lucien's attempt at levity fell on stony ground. He paused, sighed. "I just wanted to make it better for you, Sophie."

Her bitter laugh echoed around the cabin.

"Well, guess what? I didn't need your fucked up version of a fairy story to save me."

Desolation settled on his shoulders like a weightlifter's barbell. He couldn't tell her the truth. He couldn't say that something about her brittle, defensive answers about her husband at her interview had rung alarm bells in his head, or that he'd been operating on pure instinct when he'd given the order to have Daniel Black investigated. He couldn't tell her that she'd given him so much more than he'd bargained for over the last week, or that she'd changed his life just as much as he'd changed hers.

So he shrugged instead, retreating into his habitual cool demeanour. "It's better that you know. Best that you hold all the cards."

"Best?" She sprang out of her seat, backing away from him. "Best?" her voice shook as she opened the bedroom door. "Fuck off, Lucien. I don't need lessons in love from someone who knows nothing of it."

Chapter Thirty-Three

Sophie stared fixedly out of the window as Lucien eased his car to a stop outside her house. It looked somehow unfamiliar and ominous rather than like the haven it used to be. It was a little before ten, and thankfully the street seemed to be treating itself to a Sunday morning lie-in, curtains resolutely closed against the inevitably grey morning. Sophie was grateful. The last thing she wanted was an audience. Lucien in his Aston Martin stood out like a flashing beacon amongst this suburban landscape of paunchy men walking their dogs with family saloons parked on their drives.

She had no clue what to say to him. The latter part of the flight home had been hellish. After she'd seen the photos of Dan with his mistress, all she'd wanted to do was to run away and scream: instead, she'd been trapped. Lying huddled on the bed, she'd turned the events of the last week over and over in her mind. Everything she'd come to think she knew about Lucien had been wrong. He'd used her. He'd identified her as a vulnerable target and taken advantage of her to get his own sexual kicks.

"Sophie, I really am sorry." Lucien's voice was low and loaded with regret. "Upsetting you was the last thing I wanted to do."

She closed her eyes against his empty words. How could he have expected those photos to do anything but hurt her? Except it wasn't just the photographs of Dan that had hurt. Now, the fresh pain of Lucien's deceit hurt like hell on top of it all. She'd been a prize fool to let him flatter her into bed. Any last vestige of self-esteem she'd managed to hang onto had dissolved at the thought of how easily she'd been corrupted, of the things she'd allowed to happen.

"I thought it would help you."

"Help me?" She repeated his words slowly, turning them over in her mind. Because they made no sense. "Tell me, please - because I'm dying to know - how did you think showing me pictures of my husband with his mistress would help me, Lucien? Don't you think that knowing he's been seeing someone else hurts enough already?"

He sighed heavily and scrubbed his hands over his face. "I made a mistake."

"No, *I* made the mistake, and *I'm* sorry." Sophie heard the quake in her voice but she couldn't hold it steady. "I'm sorry I ever laid eyes on you." She shook her head in disgust. "As if it wasn't bad enough that my husband is having an affair. Now I've lost the only advantage I had. I'm as bad as he is."

A bitter laugh rattled through her chest. "And you know what makes it even worse, Lucien? At least Dan looks as if he has feelings for her. He might even love her for all I know." Her voice cracked and fresh tears tumbled uninvited down her cheeks. "What I've done is far, far worse. I've let some cold, calculating stranger screw me out of revenge." She choked the words out. "Screw me over, more like."

Lucien stared at her, dull-eyed, his golden skin paler than she'd ever seen it.

"You didn't do this out of revenge Sophie, you're so much better than…"

"Don't tell me what I am, Lucien," she cut across him. "You don't really know me at all, not in any way that matters. I did this to hurt my husband. It could have been anyone. It just happened to be you."

"That's a lie and you know it," he said, quietly.

"No, it isn't. Why pretty it up? You saw me as easy pickings, and I saw you as a way to get my own back. No more, no less."

She reached for the door, but his hands clamped around hers.

"Okay, Ms. Black. You've had your say. Now I'd like mine."

She stilled because he left her no other option; his hands held her, vice-like.

"Believe it or not, I really am sorry for showing you those pictures, but I'm not one bit sorry for having sex with you. You are fucking beautiful, Sophie Black, and you needed someone to remind you of it."

Sophie met his eyes in silence. Fierce frustration turned his blue irises smoky, and his body angled towards hers was rigid as stone. Only his thumbs moved, sliding over the pulse points of her wrists.

"You had sadness written all over your face the first day you walked into my office," he said softly. "I wanted to take it away. "

She wanted to look down but his eyes demanded hers. *How did he do that?* Sincerity came so easily to him, but after this morning she had no way of telling if he was just a damn good liar. Lucien had a way of looking at her that made her want to fall back in to his arms again, but wasn't that exactly what his clever words were designed to do? To reel her in then make a fool of her?

"Newsflash, hero. You haven't made things better. You've made them ten times worse."

She saw him flinch and tried to pull her hands from his, but he held her fast.

"Can you tell me you didn't enjoy all those things we did? Because I know better."

He leaned closer, and Sophie stiffened.

She didn't want him near her.

She did want him near her.

"'I know because I watched your eyes, Sophie. I watched them every time you came, and I didn't see sadness any more." His massaging thumbs were driving her crazy. "I saw joy, and I saw beauty. I saw you shine."

His raw honesty melted her anger and left her defenseless. She was suddenly tired beyond endurance, and her heart ached with sadness.

"How exactly was this supposed to end then, Lucien?"

He sighed and shook his head. "I figured I could screw you happy, I guess."

It was up there amongst the craziest, sweetest things Sophie had ever heard. How could someone so devastatingly sexy and masculine be so childlike?

"And then what? Are you planning to drop down on one knee and declare true love?" Sophie saw his jaw harden and his eyes flicker. "No, I thought not. So, let me guess… I'm supposed to go home and give Dan what for while you move on to rescue the next spurned wife?" A pulse was visible in Lucien's clenched cheek. "Am I supposed to turn up for work on Monday as if nothing happened?"

She looked out of the window at the spattering rain. He really hadn't thought this fairytale thing through. In all the stories she'd loved as a child, the knight didn't rescue the princess and then hand her right back to the evil prince.

Lucien opened his mouth to answer when she turned back to him, but then seemed to change his mind and simply shook his head with a resigned half-shrug. It was just as well. There was nothing he could offer in the way of justification.

"Grow up, Lucien. Life isn't like that."

Lucien didn't try to hold onto Sophie's hands when she eased them out of his and opened the door. He stepped out of the car too, cold drizzle dampening his face as he lifted her bag out of the boot.

He saw how Sophie's eyes were drawn to her front door. She was obviously desperate to get away from him. He couldn't blame her. Her cheeks were colourless and her eyes brimmed with regret so poignant that it hurt to look at her.

"I'll call you later?" He reached out without hope and touched the sleeve of her cherry red coat.

She shook her head, dashing the back of her hand across her eyes.

"Come to work tomorrow," he tried again, unable to keep the edge of urgency out of his voice. He needed to see her soon, just to know that she'd made it through whatever she now had to face with Dan.

"I can't, Lucien," she whispered. "You know I can't."

He touched his fingers against her cheek, wet with tears and rain.

"I don't want to leave you like this."

"You're not leaving me." Her voice steadied as she took the bag from him and stepped back. "I'm leaving you."

Lucien shoved his hands through his hair as he watched her go.

He'd screwed up.

What the fuck had he been thinking?

He should never have showed her those photographs. He'd have given anything to go back and change the last few hours. The pain in Sophie's eyes when she'd been confronted with the technicolour truth had all but torn his heart out of his body.

He now knew how his mother's face must have looked when she'd walked in on his father bent over his secretary: he'd felt like a bastard watching Sophie crumple.

A heavy sigh escaped him as he glanced at her resolutely closed door. She'd crossed back into her own world.

He thumped his fists down hard on the steering wheel as he climbed back into the driver's seat. He'd intended to send her into battle ready to rip her fuck-wit of a husband to shreds, but his shock-jock brand of pep talk had backfired badly. She wasn't battle-ready. Sophie was battered and broken before she'd even stepped into the ring, and it was all his fault.

Chapter Thirty-Four

Sophie walked through the cold, silent rooms of her house, still wearing her coat and carrying her weekend bag with the air of a visiting hotel guest.

She remembered the first time she and Dan had viewed the house, six months before their wedding. They'd fallen head over heels for it the moment they'd walked through the door. It wasn't the biggest or the flashiest, but they could make it into the perfect nest for two - or three, given time - Dan had grinned to the estate agent.

The black marble work surface in the kitchen was cool beneath her fingers. It had been beyond their modest budget really, but Dan had broken the bank to get it because Sophie had loved it so much.

She paused in the living room to study the photograph of them, taken on their wedding day. It wasn't the best photo of Sophie, but she'd awarded it pride of place because it had captured a smile of pure joy on Dan's face. Looking at it now, all she could see was that same smile on a different photo, being bestowed upon another woman.

In the bedroom, she dropped her bag on the end of the neatly made bed and perched awkwardly beside it. Of all the rooms in the house, this one felt by far the most foreboding.

Had Dan ever brought that woman here?

Had they made love in her bed?

Sophie stood up at the unsavoury thought and unbuttoned her cherry red coat slowly, then unzipped her bag. She needed to unpack, to wash Norway and Lucien Knight out of her clothes and her mind.

She shook out her best dress and held it against her. It needed to be dry cleaned to remove the flecks of creamy pannacotta that stood out starkly against the black silk. Sophie gripped the dress, winded by the memory of last night in Lucien's dining room. Had it really been less than twenty-four hours ago? It felt like a lifetime.

When she reached down into her bag again, her fingers bumped against something she didn't expect to find there. Something hard. She frowned and pushed the clothes aside, then gasped softly. A shallow, black box about the length of a shoebox lay at the bottom of her bag. A box with the all too familiar Knight Inc. logo engraved in gunmetal grey on the top.

Sophie sucked in a sharp breath and sat down again. What was inside? She drew it out and balanced it carefully on her knees. It was heavier than she'd expected, and she was sure that whatever it held wouldn't help her to put Lucien out of her head. She should hide it in the bottom of her wardrobe without looking inside. Or even better, throw it straight into the bin.

She opened the box.

Her fingers shook as she peeled back the crisp black tissue paper within. A card lay on top, thick, creamy and inscribed with Lucien's bold black handwriting.

Your three wishes.
9am on Monday.
Be there.
Lucien

Sophie knew exactly what lay amongst the folds of the tissue paper, but withdrew the objects one by one anyway.

A wisp of black lace and silk.

The heavy silver acorn, suddenly duller and tawdry.

The aurora glass dildo, robbed of its rainbows and glitter by the oppressive London skies and Sophie's mood.

They all looked so ordinary, so mundane, here in her orderly bedroom. Maybe Lucien had been the magician whose touch had brought them to life. As she sighed and folded back the tissue to return them to their box, something else caught her eye nestled at the bottom.

She picked up the small, gold velvet box, vintage, if the well-loved condition of the fabric was any indicator. Soft and worn, Sophie knew instantly that somebody had cherished its contents enough to hold it often.

Her fingers curled over the edges and clutched it tightly. Warm and tactile in her palm, Sophie could only wonder at what lay inside, and why Lucien had wanted her to have it.

She unfurled her fingers and lifted the hinged lid slowly. A folded slip of paper fluttered onto her lap, then she saw that inside the box lay a delicate gold bracelet, its links interspersed every now and then with a small round jewel. Each diamond flashed aurora-bright as she held it up to the light to study it. She caught her breath. It was stunning, as if someone had reached up and captured tiny flecks of the brilliant Norwegian night sky.

But it wasn't just the beauty of the bracelet that mesmerised her. Sophie recognised it. She'd seen it once before.

Or rather she'd seen a photograph of someone wearing it.

Lucien's mother. It had been around her wrist in the photograph on Lucien's desk.

Sophie held back the tears that threatened to start again as she looked at the delicate, treasured jewels. The sex toys had been unexpected, but she wasn't really surprised to have found them there.

But this... why? It must be precious to him. She laid the bracelet carefully back in its box and reached for the note.

Another strong and beautiful woman loved this very much. May it always remind you how big the world is, and that you always have a choice.
Remember, Princess.

L x

Sophie read the words over again and shook her head gently. Just when she thought she had Lucien Knight all figured out, he turned right around and did something so unashamedly romantic that she wished he was there so she could look into his eyes and see the truth he wouldn't have been able to hide.

She fastened the clasp of the bracelet around her wrist, watching as the tiny stones cast rainbow shades on her skin. And then, second by second, minute by minute, Sophie simply sat and remembered.

She remembered vast kaleidoscope skies, snow-capped mountains, and glittering fjords.

She remembered warm fur at her back, and cold champagne on her tongue. And she remembered the dark, intricate lone wolf that slumbered across the beautiful shoulders of the man who'd taken the time to shown her how big the world truly is.

Lost in her thoughts, Sophie flinched at the sudden sound from downstairs of the front door banging shut. Footsteps and a dragged suitcase on the wooden hall floor heralded Dan's return. She caught her breath and quickly packed Lucien's three wishes away in the black box.

It was time to go into battle.

In the blue corner, her husband. The man she'd planned to love forever.

In the red corner, her lover. The man she hadn't planned on loving at all.

Sophie faltered, feeling exposed and alone.

Did she actually love either of them? Did either of them love her?

"Sophie? Dan's urgent voice carried up the stairs. "Soph, are you up there?"

She crossed to the wardrobe and quickly slipped the black box into a space at the back, then clicked the door quietly closed.

"Just coming," she called, amazed that her voice sounded calm and clear. With one last glance down at the bracelet on her wrist, she opened the bedroom door and headed for the stairs.

And that was when someone banged hard on the front door.

Sophie froze, halfway down the staircase, her eyes on her husband's familiar suit-clad back as he turned the latch on the door.

Fleetingly, she admired his thoroughness in remembering to wear business dress, even though she knew he hadn't been near a meeting. *Very convincing, Dan.*

She knew who was outside. It was inevitable.

Dan swung the door back and glared at the stranger lounging cross-armed against the doorjamb.

"Whatever you're selling, we don't need it," he said irritably.

The stranger stared at him and said nothing.

A long moment passed. Sophie sensed that Dan was about to try to close the door. She knew just as certainly that the visitor would prevent it.

She broke the silence.

"He isn't selling anything." Sophie spoke softly but distinctly, glancing from one man to the other.

Dan turned enquiring eyes in her direction. Whether she was ready or not, it seemed that the fighters were coming out of their corners regardless.

Was she supposed to referee between them? How could she? Her loyalties were divided between the man she'd married for better or worse, and the beautiful Viking who'd turned her world upside down.

"He's Lucien." She swallowed hard. Seconds out. Sophie could almost hear the bell ringing.

"He's Lucien Knight.

To be continued...

Lucien and Sophie's story concludes in book two of the Knight Erotic Romance series, Knight and Stay, available now.

ABOUT THE AUTHOR

USA Today best selling author Kitty French lives in the UK with her husband and their two little boys.

Kitty also writes steamy romantic comedy under the pseudonym Kat French. Undertaking Love is out now from HarperCollins.

SIGN UP FOR KITTY'S NEWSLETTER:
If you'd like to receive news and snippets about Kitty's upcoming books, please email on kittyfrenchwriter@me.com to join the mailing list.

GET IN TOUCH WITH KITTY
Twitter: @kittysbooks
Facebook: Kitty French
Email: kittyfrenchwriter@me.com
Website: www.kittyfrench.com

ACKNOWLEDGMENTS

I've had such a ball writing this book, and I must say thank you to some people who have helped me enormously along the way.

I owe huge thanks to Charlie Hobson, my dream editor and smut sister extraordinaire. It's been a pleasure to work together, let's do it again soon.

To Angela Oltmann of Angie-O-Creations, thank you so much for all of your hard work on the cover for Knight & Play – you took my garbled vision and turned it into something that I love so much that it makes me want to lick the screen!

To the beautiful Minxes, my writing bezzies and all round cool ladies – you rock, thank you for holding my hand from conception to publication. I wouldn't have been brave enough without you.

Special thanks to Sally Clements for being a formatting genius!

Thanks also to the lovely Bob girls for unfailingly waving your pompoms, and for reading the book as I wrote it and encouraging me on. Special thanks to Loulou for coming to the rescue with the perfect title.

And last but by no means least, thank you to my family, my gorgeous husband most of all. Where would I be without you? One day we'll go to Norway and watch those lights together.

Printed in Great Britain
by Amazon.co.uk, Ltd.,
Marston Gate.